NATHANAEL LESSORE

HOT
KEY
BOOKS

First published in Great Britain in 2023 by
HOT KEY BOOKS
4th Floor, Victoria House, Bloomsbury Square
London WC1B 4DA
Owned by Bonnier Books
Sveavägen 56, Stockholm, Sweden
www.hotkeybooks.com

A CIP catalogue record for this book is available from the British Library.

ISBN: 978-1-4714-1322-3
Also available as an ebook and in audio

5

This book is typeset using Atomik ePublisher
Printed and bound in Great Britain by Clays Ltd, Elcograf S.p.A.

Hot Key Books is an imprint of Bonnier Books UK
www.bonnierbooks.co.uk

For OGC

Inducing Me

My name is Shaun Thompson, but people call me Growls because I growl like a tiger before my rhymes.

Yeah they call me Growls,
I'm like a tiger on the prowl.
King of jungles so you better take a bow.
King of concrete so you better say it loud.

You best believe there's more where that came from. Man's got bars for days, like a prison or a vending machine, you feel me?

It's Monday morning so I'm in my form group. Can't lie, I'm one of the top thirty students in my class. But I've figured out how to stand out from the crowd and get Tanisha to notice me. The minute she clocks my rap skills, I know she'll be super on it.

I'm sat next to Shanks, my partner in grime, but the space next to him is empty, because only the cool kids sit at the back. Shanks is legit my OG. Swear down, he's had my back since day. His mum and my mum started chatting outside the gates when we were in primary school. Then Mrs Shanks sometimes took me to their house after school if my mum was working late, shout out receptionist jobs. The first time I went to his yard, I didn't wanna leave. Man had kitchen tiles and matching curtains on some interior-design wave, and his garden was a private one, not even for the whole block. What got me most though was when his mum said we were eating lamb for dinner, I thought it was gonna be in some kinda kebab shape, but this thing was on the bone. She called it lamb shanks for her little lamb, and that's how Shanks got his nickname, Little Lamb. But people at school mocked it when I called him that, so we changed it to Lamb Shanks (Shanks for short).

Me and Shanks, we been tight ever since. It wasn't too long after that when I decided that we should become a rap duo. He weren't super on it at first, but he saw the light. I told Shanks that people would sing our names from mountaintops, where milk flows like honey and goat farmers sing Christmas carols in the midwinter. I was gonna make enough money to get the real cereal, and not the one with the fake bumblebee that doesn't even have a name.

You could say Shanks' MC skills aren't levels with mine,

but he's mad smart. And wise, like one of those talking owls from a cartoon. He taught me that 'banoffee pie' is called that because it's a mix of 'banana' and 'toffee'. And last week he gave me good advice on how to finally make Tanisha my number one.

'If you put Vaseline on your eyelashes, it'll make them look longer,' he said. I guess it would have worked, except I used half a tub and the school sent me home because it looked like I had an eye infection. But none of that matters now. When I'm a famous rapper, I won't have to worry about getting girls to like me. They'll see that I've got loads of bars and money. Man, rappers are so lucky that they can buy anything they want and not worry about their mum saying 'no'.

'Yeah, but being rich and famous would make you lonely because you'd be living in a big house by yourself,' Shanks whispers to me while our form tutor takes the register, and I guess he has got a point. I think that's why they've got all those girls by the pool popping bottles, it means they've always got someone to talk to. Big mansions are always the first ones to get haunted too.

Imagine having all that money though. You could eat food with more than three ingredients all the time, buy clothes that fit you perfectly, and you wouldn't have to worry about turning everything off at the plug to save electricity. Shanks don't get it; I definitely seen him leaving rooms without turning the light off. And I'm sure his mum doesn't have to count the prices of everything when she's shopping like it's a science test or something. The struggle is real out here, like when my Aunt Tina oils up her waist to put on skinny jeans.

The bell for first period goes and we head to English with Mr Rix. At the back of this class is where we write our sickest bars and practise freestyle battles. Sometimes Shanks spits his bars quieter when there's people about, but that's only because of copyright issues.

Can't lie, writing bars in English is one of my favourite things about this subject. But the best thing about this lesson isn't here yet. I'm waiting for her to arrive, and I'm concentrating hard on the door so I don't miss her.

'Growls, why you frowning like that?' Shanks asks. 'Did a moth get stuck in your ear again?'

'No, I ain't got a moth in my ear.' This guy has a vivid imagination – it was just your average beetle. He asks me if I have a spare pen but I can't respond. Tanisha just walked in and I'm bare distracted. She's parted her hair to the left today, and her eye make-up has those little wings on them. Shanks rolls his eyes but I don't care. Today's the day.

'Fam, you say that every day. The last time she actually talked to you, you got nervous and dropped your chicken bake on her shoe.' Shanks is a liar. He wasn't even there when it happened.

4

Tanisha and her friends always sit near us at the back. This one time I pulled out a chair for her to sit down, but she just laughed and carried on walking. Swear down, this girl needs to chill. Shanks would've liked Tanisha sitting with us, he's always tryna get people to sit with us. But if it's not Tanisha, then I ain't interested. She's so popular her phone is always going off, but she don't care. She's so cool that sometimes she doesn't even check it, even though it could be an emergency. The only people that ever call *me* are Shanks and sometimes his mum to ask me if Shanks is at my yard. I wish Tanisha would call me though, that would give me life.

'Shanks, I ain't playing. I really think today's the day. What's the worst she could say?' I ask.

'That she won't go out with you because you have dry elbows, your ears stick out and sometimes after PE you smell like an onion.'

'OK, that would be kinda next if she said that. Bro, why you shooting down my confidence? You know I bruise easily, so be careful when you handle me.'

'Bruv, I ain't handling you in any way, stop being weird.' Now he's getting defensive. I'm telling you, this is how it always goes.

'It was a simile,' I explain.

'No, it wasn't – if anything it was a metaphor. A simile is when something is like something.'

'So a simile is like a metaphor. Stop confusing me, bruv, you're putting me off. I'm supposed to be talking to Tanisha.'

'Why don't you just use your bars to get her digits?'

I think he's right. Spitting bars is one of the most romantic things an MC can do. And when she finally realises how talented I am, she won't notice that I got four Subway stains on my shirt. OK, this is it. I do the breath test where I breathe into my hand and if it doesn't make me light-headed, then I'm good to go. This is kinda exciting. I can't believe I'm doing this. It's like my mind won't believe my brain.

Just as I'm about to make my move, Mr Rix starts the lesson. I know he's a bit of neek, but Mr Rix is a decent teacher. He teaches us big words like 'derelict' and 'invaluable'.

'Settle down, everybody. Today I want to do a little articulation exercise. As you know, we'll be looking at autobiographies this term.' He wants us to write about robots? 'The literal translation of autobiography is "history of the self".' Oh. Cool. I was half right – robots might wanna write about theirselves too. 'So before we start,' Mr Rix says, 'I want you each to tell me an interesting fact about yourself that you could mention in your autobiography.'

I look at Shanks. How is this guy gonna say 'before we start' and then ask us to do stuff? Fam, that *is* the start. I don't go to football and say, 'Before we start, I'm gonna bang in five goals.'

Ryan, some next guy who always has a dead trim, is the first to stand.

'Well, I'm not sure if this counts, but my dad was in the circus, and when I was younger he taught me how to ride a unicycle. Sometimes I use it to go to the shop around the corner from my house.' Well done, this guy knows how to ride half a bike.

Stephanie goes next. She would be pretty decent, but she switched on me once for no reason, just because I accidentally got chewing gum in both our eyebrows. I found it stuck under the desk, but it was watermelon flavour which is nasty. When I flicked it off my finger, some went in my face, and when I tried again with the rest, it went on hers too.

'So, I can actually speak five different languages,' she says. What's the point? You only live in one country.

Everyone's going around talking about moist things they've done, like meeting celebrities or swimming with dolphins or whatever. Dolphins are just bald sharks and celebrities are boring anyway; when I met Idris Elba outside Greggs, he kept running away saying, 'I'm not Idris Elba, leave me alone, I don't even look like him.' Never meet your heroes, that's all I'm sayin'.

It finally gets to my turn and I don't know what to say. Maybe I could tell them about the time I met Idris Elba. Or the time I did over seven kick-ups. There's too much to choose from. But Tanisha is watching me, and I need to impress her. If I'm gonna do this dead task for Mr Rix, I might as well do some trademark acrobatic lyrics and get that love train rollin'.

'I can MC off the dome,' I say, standing up. I hear a couple people groan, but they groaned at Ludacris when he flew into the sun, and nothing stopped him achieving his dreams. Shanks is looking down at the floor, it's the head angle for optimum audio quality. Tanisha's not even watching me, she's on her phone. If my juicy hot bars don't impress her, I don't know what will. Mr Rix just looks confused.

It's now or never.

'Yo, spitting bars out here, that's my big plan.
See you nod along, you a big fan.
Fan-tastic say it twice coz I cancan.
Getting hench, I'm a classic version of a roadman.
I know man, I know man well.
I know well . . . Wait . . . Emmanuel?'

Damn, I dropped it. But even heart surgeons have bad days at the office, it ain't a big deal. Tanisha weren't even paying attention anyway. Two people start clapping, and Mr Rix looks even more confused than before.

He says, 'Thanks, Shaun, I think we'll leave it there.'

'Wait, sir, I can do better.' It can't end like this. I'm usually on point, but Tanisha was making me nervous. 'Mr Rix, if you drop a beat, I swear, like, I can stay on beat.' Some of the class are grinning at each other. Mr Rix just says that we don't have time and we should move on. I guess the battle is lost, like the one at Waterloo station.

The rest of the lesson is calm. I start thinking about my autobiography, like, if Sherlock Homes can write one about his houses, I could do one that's way less boring. It would have to be a side hustle to my rap career, but imagine all the P that I would make.

When the lesson finishes and we start packing our books away, I see Shanks look past me, and his mouth is hanging open. I turn to see what he's looking at. OMG it's Tanisha, she's actually coming over. She must have noticed that I've started doing press-ups. Every now and then, I try to work out almost twice a week, coz it's important to exercise your triceratops, your lorax and your Lithuania. When you put the work in and come out looking like a snack, man can't be surprised when people wanna gobble-gobble. Shanks sits nearby, pretending to put stuff in his bag so that he doesn't interrupt us. True wingman out here.

'I liked your rap. Please tell me you were being ironic.' When she speaks it's like drill music to my ears. My days, she's so pretty.

'Ha. Ironic. I don't even know the meaning of the word,' I reply, which is true because I really don't. She's not saying anything. She just pulls out her phone and starts playing with her hair like she's waiting for me to say something. 'Yo, is your head itchy? Because my mum's got this shampoo for dry or itchy scalps.' I know that because it's written on the bottle and I memorised it.

'What are you saying? That I got a dry scalp?' She stops playing with her hair and folds her arms.

'No, you were just touching your hair and I thought maybe it was itching. Like, don't worry or nothing, it's medicinal.' She picks up her handbag and dashes her phone inside, then she gives me a proper screw face and storms out. Like, legit what just happened? It was going so well. I look over at Shanks, who saw the whole thing, bare hurt.

'Shanks, I was just trying to help.'

'I know,' he sighs.

'Bruv, it was medicinal.'

'I know.'

I spend the rest of the day wishing I'll bump into Tanisha, so I can tell her that her hair ain't dry and that. It's beautiful, soft, and damp like when Shanks' mum cooks banana bread. But it's 3.30 p.m. and I'm losing hope. The bell's gone, and Shanks had to rush off. His mum took him bowling and it's not even his birthday.

Oh my days, I see her. She's almost on her way out the gates, and I have to run to catch up with her and her friends. One of them says something as I approach, and they all start laughing. Tanisha tells them to go wait for her at the bus stop, and they walk off, linking their arms and rolling their eyes. I don't care that they laughed. Adrian, my big brother from the same mother, taught me that sticks and stones can break my bones but words can only leave emotional scars that others can't see. Tanisha is so pretty, even when she's angry. When her frown is intense and her mouth gets all pouty, it makes me tingle like Miles Morales' spider-sense.

'What do you want? Come to tell me more about my bad hair?'

'No, I come to tell you that your hair's really nice and your face is nice and I'm really sorry. I didn't want to upset you before.' I'm shaking a little bit, but that's just coz my street-dance training is on high alert, not because I'm nervous.

She rolls her eyes. 'Give me your phone.' Tanisha holds out her hand. I give it to her. She quickly taps numbers in and shoves the phone back at me. 'Don't make me regret that,' she says.

Hah, 'regret'. I don't fully know the meaning of that word either. She goes off towards the bus stop to join her friends. I run home to call Shanks and tell him what just happened. Don't ever doubt me, bruv, I got game. I got so many girls' numbers that if you line them up back-to-back it would be well confusing, even for a mathsmagician.

2

They Call Me the Athlete Coz of My Athlete's Foot

We're doing PE off-site in Catford at one of those sports tracks with all the lines that you see on the Olympics. It's like a big stretched-out circle with grass in the middle. Mr Youssef has got us running 4,000 meters, which is pretty useless because in the real world you can just get the bus. I'm sweating like a Krispy Kreme and my thigh gap keeps rubbing together. Tanisha and her friends are way ahead, so me and Shanks are running behind everyone else so we can talk in private.

'What you gonna message her?' Shanks is grilling me like a baked potato while he runs alongside me.

'Chill, bruh. They don't call me Cassava for nothing.' I guess that's half-true.

'Growls, cassava's a root. I think you mean Casanova.'

'I think I mean supernova, because that's what I am.'

'Whatever. It's just that the last date you went on didn't really work out that well. Remember Nadia?' Why's he got to bring that up? Nadia was peak. We went on one date and she never spoke to me again.

'That's because you sneezed on her.'

'I sneezed *near* her.'

'OK fine, but you got some on her and your nose was bleeding.'

'My nose was only bleeding because that stupid football hit me in the face.'

'You kicked that ball into your own face.'

'Bruv, you know I wasn't wearing the right shoes. And who pumps a football up that much? The thing was rock solid.' Swear down, that football was a weapon of match destruction. I still don't get why Nadia was so upset.

'Come on, you were trying to impress her and it flopped.'

You know what? This guy is stressing me out. Why we talking about Nadia when I'm trying to think of what to message Tanisha? 'Bro, you don't know what's in my heart,' I tell him. 'And why you bringing up old wounds right now? You know I got postal dramatic stress disorder.' We carry on running in silence for a bit.

'Aite, I'm sorry, I won't bring her up any more.' Shanks tries to put his arm around me, but I run sideways a little bit so he can't reach. I'm not ready to be touched. Mr Youssef

13

notices us way behind everyone else so he shouts at us to pick up the pace. He doesn't know that me and Shanks are already supreme athletes and we don't wanna make those other pedestrians in our class look bad.

'What do you think I should do with Tanisha then?' I have to ask him because no one else in our year knows me the way he does, or ever really talks to us on a level. I would go to Adrian, but last time I asked him to help me find a girl, he just held up a mirror. Shanks isn't on that wave like I am, but I don't mind because I'm my best self when I'm with him, he's the perfect hypeman. You know what, he really *is* the perfect hypeman, and that gives me an idea.

'Shanks?'

'Yeah, fam.'

'What if I link Tanisha and you come with?' Why didn't I think of it before? With Shanks there, he can talk me up, and we always have fun together. Maybe Tanisha will see that and get gassed and she'll join in the bants. He thinks about it for a sec and says that I'm less likely to injure myself if he comes with. We're in.

Mr Youssef tells us to hurry up again, we've fallen way behind now. Shanks is such a neek, he starts running faster and faster, but I'm at optimal capacity. When you're a Scorpio like me, we have explosive speed but less stamina. Shanks has already started overtaking people. He's killing it.

By the time I get to my last lap, everyone else is finished and they're all lying there out of breath. You see me, yeah, I was smart and I conserved all my energy till the end. I kick my legs into overdrive and I'm proper sprinting now. Literally, I'm running so fast I must be a blur. I think Mr Youssef is calling at me to hurry. I can't hear him though, because that old man on the lawnmower is overtaking me.

When I cross the finish line, most people have already gone to the changing rooms. Shanks is waiting for me, even though he finished third out of everyone, which is kinda sick when you think that we were behind for so long. He says he had time to sit down and catch his breath while I was on my final lap.

'So you saw my final lap?' I ask him. 'Be real, how insanely fast was I going?'

'I think I saw a butterfly land on you.'

Me and Shanks are in the changing rooms at school. We didn't change in Catford, because we ran out of time. Apparently someone made us late and we had to get back. It's calm because we don't really like using the changing rooms when they're too packed anyway. Man get too rowdy, and I have to suck my belly in when I'm changing T-shirts. I type a message to Tanisha asking her to go cinema, and spend the rest of the day avoiding her in case she doesn't reply.

* * *

Why she airing me like a cupboard? We're in geography
class the next day, and I can see her see me. I guess the vibe
ain't right, geography is dead, fam. Our teacher won't even
teach us real geography stuff, like where to find the lost city
of Atlanta, or where the wild things are. Maybe she's not
talking to me coz people were mocking it when I said that
a stalactite is when two stalacs are best friends.

Shanks notices that I keep checking my phone and looking
over, so I just lock and keep it in my pocket.

Swear down, Tanisha owes me an apology,
We found ourselves in geography, it's not for me,
You can ghost but I'm a gangsta living and I been studying
G-ology.

Those bars were tighter than two stalacs, a bit like me
and Shanks when we share a milkshake.

The bell goes and I wanna go chat to her, but my heart
is beating too fast like drum and bass, and for some reason
my legs won't move; maybe I been sitting down for too
long and I got peas and noodles in my legs.

Shanks tries to encourage me, but the moment's gone.
Or is it?

As we're walking out, I can see a pen on the table where she
was sitting. She's one of those people who writes stuff down
in class. I tell Shanks not to wait for me before next lesson.

OK, there's Tanisha and I have her pen. I don't need to be

16

nervous, what if the inventor of paracetamol was nervous? He would have never invented Paris. This is a pressurised situation, a bit like when you go to the optician and they test your spelling. I'm telling you it's a hoax, the words they make you spell are always made up.

'Yo, Tanisha.' Why are her friends always laughing? My leg was numb when I stood up, but I styled it out by pretending to tie my shoelace. Bare people tie their shoes lying down on the floor, it ain't that deep. 'I got your pen, I thought you might need it.' I climb back onto my feet like I normally stand because balance game strong now. She tells her friends that she'll link up with them later.

'That's not my pen,' she says, and then she sighs.

'So did you get my message?' I ask. The trick is not to look desperate.

'I did, but you know what it's like. I've been so busy, getting my nails done and my eyebrows threaded and making content and that.'

'Yeah, I seen how many followers you got on IG, you must be really busy trying to keep up with them. I'm busy too though, hustling and being a G on road and that.'

'You think I got a lot of followers?' She smiles and looks at the floor. 'Because I wasn't sure if it's enough. I wanna be an influencer.' OMG she's responding to me like we're equals. I can't gas her up too much.

'Are you kidding? You've got bare followers, you're gonna

go far in life.' I can't help it, she's life goals. 'One day I'm gonna have as many as you, and have this huge squad, and they'll respect my gangsta vibe because I'll have enough money to buy them all ice cream. Every. Single. One of them.' Tanisha's pulled out her phone and is literally on the gram right now, admiring her own selfies. I rate that. 'I just need to get on your level of socials,' I tell her. Me and Shanks only have fifty followers when we combine. Most of mine are family members, but Imma unfollow them when I make it big. Too much dead weight. Most people at school don't follow us back, which I get because me and Shanks are before our time like jetlag or an analogue watch.

Tanisha looks up and nods slowly. 'OK, let's go out, one time, and just see how it goes. I don't know what I'm thinking,' she says. We quickly make plans to meet at Peckham cinema on Saturday, and then I literally run away before she can change her mind. As I'm sprinting down the corridor, I can tell that my road energy sealed the deal (I don't know why seals are so good at deals) and the first thing I do is find Shanks.

'We're in,' I tell him.

'We're in what?'

I tell him about my chat with Tanisha, and how I was so gangsta that she just crumbled at the knees and asked me out.

Back at mine, I'm trying on different outfits to wear for my date on Saturday. Shanks came over after school because he likes being my stylist. Mum is in the kitchen on the phone looking stressed. Shanks gives her a quick wave, but my trick is to avoid direct contact when she's on one. I hear her moaning about the cost of living and having to cut back, which is peak because we already been making cutbacks. Our toothpaste got one of those clips you put on food packets to keep them fresh – we use it to squeeze all the last drops out. And last time I asked her for one-fiddy for trainers, she gave me 50p for materials to start building my own pair.

Adrian is here too, I can hear music from his room. He's a little bit hench, like a semi-pro badminton player or an under-sixteens footballer. When we pass him in the corridor, he's wearing a loose tank top and sliders, looking like an uncle in a car park on a hot day.

Me and Shanks spend the rest of the afternoon in my room trying on clothes for my date with Tanisha. I got this one T-shirt with bare holes that I can pretend are on purpose, but one of the holes is right over my nipple and I don't want babies to get the wrong idea. My other favourite T-shirt is a plain blue one, but it's got a grease stain on the chest that never comes off. I can wear it if I keep my arms folded the whole time, but that means I can't do normal things like tie my laces, or high-five people on escalators, or pick lavender or whatever. In the end, we do what we always do, which is that Shanks will lend me a top and I have to give it back later.

3

Man's Proper Date (Not the Cockroach Fruit)

When we rock up to the cinema on Saturday, Tanisha's already outside. Look at her, standing there, all confident like she just won the Oscar for best album. Shanks is rubbing my shoulders like I'm a boxer in a bathrobe, telling me that I got this and it's gonna be the best date. He's paying for my ticket, but he didn't mention money for snacks so I brought some from home. The only thing we had in our fridge was yogurt, strawberry on some five-a-day wave, and I hijacked a pot and three spoons from the drawer. I have to hurry back after the film so my mum doesn't notice the spoons are missing.

As we get closer to Tanisha, she smiles when she recognises me, but she stops smiling and looks confused when she spots Shanks.

'Oh, I thought it was just gonna be the two of us,' she says. Boy, she does not look happy to see him.

'Nah, the thing is yeah, I ain't the kinda guy to leave my friends behind. When you're an MC duo like we are –' me and Shanks quickly do our signature back-to-back pose – 'we ain't bout to leave each other out of a cinema trip.' Now that she knows I'm a good friend, she probably fancies me even more. She pulls a bit of a face and walks off into the cinema.

When we catch up with her at the counter, Tanisha turns to me.

'Well?'

'Well, what?' I ask.

'Well, what film are we watching?' Oh. I didn't even look at the films, I was too busy stealing spoons and yogurt from my own yard. I ask the woman behind the counter what's the next film to start. There's a superhero film on in ten minutes, or a kids' film called *Princess Power II* that's starting now. I tell the woman that we want to watch the action film, and she looks down at the three of us and asks if we're here with an adult.

'I can call my mum,' Shanks says and he pulls out his phone. 'I'm sure she wouldn't mind.'

'Do *not* call your mum,' Tanisha says, barging past us. She tells the woman that we'll just go and see the kids' film, muttering something about 'It's bad enough he's here, allow having his mum with us.' She kinda has a point, like, who goes on a date and brings their best friend's mum? Shanks needs to get it under control; his mum ain't even a vibe, she keeps fudge in her handbag.

We order the tickets and Tanisha asks me if I'm getting snacks.

'Don't worry, I got you,' I tell her, and pat my rucksack with the yogurt inside.

'Oh thank God, I was wondering what you had in there,' she says as we follow her to the screen. When we sit down, I try to wait for Shanks to go first so that me and Tanisha can sit next to each other and hold hands maybe. But she sat down quickly and Shanks didn't clock my plan, so now it's a bit awkward because he's in the middle. Tanisha's bare tutting every time she looks at him, and I'm starting to think she don't rate him that much. I nudge him with my leg to swap places, and he tries to shuffle underneath me while I go over the top. I can feel people looking at us, but I'm doing my best to ignore them. I'm kinda sitting on Shanks' lap and we carry on shuffling, accidentally kicking the people in front of us and knocking over my rucksack, until I land in the seat next to Tanisha. I'm a little out of breath, but it's cool, I don't think she noticed.

The film starts and all the parents shush their kids. Hopefully they don't wile out, so me and Tanisha can enjoy our perfect date. The film is kinda sick though. Princess

Buttercup is trapped in a tower like 5G and her kingdom is under attack from Krumpus, some wasteman wizard who wouldn't last a day in the ends without his powers. Yo, the princess is calm though, she's rolling with some next homies who are these forest creatures and they ain't having it. Me and Shanks are invested, boy.

When there's a singing break for Princess Buttercup to wish for true love's kiss, no cap it's a sly tune, I pull out the yogurt pot and spoons to hand out. Shanks is licking his lips as I open it.

'Stay bless,' he says as we start digging in, but Tanisha's arms are folded. I hold it out for her, but she doesn't even move.

'Are you actually serious?' she hisses. She's giving the yogurt a dirty look like it's some kinda moist apricot flavour or something. As if I would bring an apricot yogurt to the cinema.

'Man brought one yogurt pot, not even on a joke ting.' She's shaking her head. 'Don't you have anything normal, like sweets or Maltesers?' she asks. What am I, Charlie and the Chocolate Factory? This girl is moving bare ungrateful.

'Bruv, if you don't want my snacks, you should have got some for yourself,' I tell her.

'I was going to order snacks but you told me not to.' She's whispering proper loud. 'I don't want to be eating yogurt with you while I'm in a cinema surrounded by kids.'

I don't get why she's so embarrassed about eating yogurt with little children around, I'm sure they won't judge her.

As the film carries on, the Krumpus is actually moving suspect. Man like Princess Buttercup better come through.

I kinda wanna make a move on Tanisha, but I'm tryna be subtle. I yawn really loudly and bring my arm up to put around her shoulder, but it turns into a real yawn and I forget what I was tryna do with it. Now I can't fake another one because she's gonna think I'm proper bored, which I'm not because this film is next level. I can sense that she's on it though, my time will come.

Halfway through the film, I'm on the edge of my seat, because I spilled my yogurt and I'm trying not to sit in it. Princess Buttercup has finally mastered her rainbow magic and she's going hard. Man does not want to return to her tower, boy, she's ready for a scrap. She acts all kind and innocent, but deep down we know she's bare ratchet.

Tanisha don't look like she's enjoying herself. Man's got her phone out, texting. I catch Shanks looking at me and he widens his eyes and starts mouthing something. I don't know what he's trying to say, but he keeps nodding towards her. I finally get it. I lean over to whisper to Tanisha.

'Yo, Tanisha?' She looks up. 'Can you put your phone away? We tryna watch the film and the light from your screen is bare distracting.' She's huffing and she rolls her eyes, but she puts her phone in her pocket and folds her arms.

The film finishes and me and Shanks are hyped. That princess was on one. When it turned out that her real power was true love, and all them woodland creatures stood up against the Krumpus, it was curtains. Ain't nobody can touch rainbow magic in the right hands, you ain't finessing that. Princess Buttercup is thug goals out here.

Rainbow magic un-mess-withable,
Cinderella vibez can't mess with a ball,
Tanisha on her phone like she gon mess with call,
Why deny my cinema vibe, with yogurt so edible?
No need for red ink for it to be ink-redible.

Tanisha missed all of it. She went toilet twenty minutes before the end and we're waiting for her outside.

'Bruv, the way all she had to do was believe in herself to unlock her magic, I'm telling you that's us with the rapping,' I say.

Shanks looks away.

'I lie?' I look at my watch and back at the door of the cinema. The last people have left and there's still no sign of Tanisha. Shanks can read my mind like the back of a shampoo bottle, and he offers to buy me an ice cream. I take one more look at my phone and at the cinema, bare longingly and that. I can't get too invested in the feels, that ain't gangsta. It's calm, Shanks said he'll pay the 20p for extra sprinkles.

Rapping My Gift to You

Tanisha messaged when she got home yesterday. Apparently she had an emergency dentist appointment, so at least she had a good reason. Shout-out dentists, those guys deserve a crown.

I need to forget Tanisha though, because today's the day that things change for me and Shanks. We're going to enter Raptology, step one to becoming famous rappers. The Akinyemi Foundation has this rap battle event for thirteen to sixteen-year-olds every summer, and this is the first year we can legally enter. I went last year and it was sick. You basically do three rounds of head-to-head, winners go through and losers go home. Or I guess the losers can stay if they're enjoying themselves, there's refreshments and that, and it might be too early for them to go home coz this is a daytime thing. I been following all the past winners on IG, and I think I saw one of them say that he got a week of studio time at the end when he won. I can already imagine Tanisha's face when she sees us dropping our fresh MC Squared tracks like Hansel and Gretel.

The competition's on 31st July so we've still got a couple months to practise. Shanks thinks it's a good idea to film ourselves doing a freestyle so we can see what we look like and come up with ways to improve. Obviously I think we're already wavey enough, but I guess it can't hurt to perfect our perfection.

He comes over after lunch, and we're in my room setting up his phone. I'm letting Shanks do our online entry because he's better at all that admin. True story, I used to think that 'admin' was short for 'adminton'. He's taking bare long though, so I tell him to skip all that useless information stuff and just put our names in. He enters our details on the site, and now I'm proper gassed, I just wanna get started on the freestyles. We shouldn't be interrupted; Adrian has football training on Sundays, and Mum's in the kitchen plotting my downfall or whatever she does in her spare time. She lost her job as a receptionist in a GP surgery a few months ago after they had to cut back on staff. I wanted her to get a job in TK Maxx and get a discount, but now she's started working nights as a cleaner, and it's peak for me and Adrian because she's always in a bad mood.

My room is just a single bed with a desk and a TV for my PlayStation, one of them old ones that has a mega back and a 12-inch frame around it. Adrian's room is way bigger, he could swing a cat if he wanted to, like if we had a cat, or a sausage dog or a small kangaroo. He wouldn't, because nobody wants that kind of heat from the are-yes-PC-yay. I used to have more things in my room, but Mum's been selling a whole load of our stuff online. Yesterday I went to sit in my desk chair and caught air because I didn't realise it weren't there no more. Next she'll be coming for my bed and I'll have to sleep on the floor like a snake.

The walls in here are peeling and there's ceiling stains, but I can Photoshop those out for the video. Don't tell Shanks, but as I'm setting up the phone, I see that Tanisha's online, so I make an executive decision to go live with this ting. When she sees the hustle, she's gonna be calling me non-stop to go on another date. We can go somewhere fancy, like Nando's or Pizza Express, where they give you extra ketchup for free and the napkins don't come out a dispenser.

'Come on, bro, are we ready? You're taking your time,' Shanks says. He's biting his nails and says he just wants to start so we can get it over with. I rate his enthusiasm, still. I quickly make a pile of cooking books that I stole from the kitchen so I can prop the phone up, hands-free, you feel me? Once it's recording, I pull my hood up and take a step back so we're both in the video.

'Yo, I'm Growls, I'm here with my G, Shanks, and together we are MC Squared,' I tell the camera.

'What? No. Cut.' Shanks doesn't like that. 'We didn't discuss names. Don't say that.'

'Aite, cool, fam, let's just continue.' He doesn't realise we're live on the internet and I wanna get past this quickly.

'No, Growls, you always do this. Do you know how it makes me feel when you make a decision for both of us without consulting me? If I'm gonna do this with you, I need to feel valued. Otherwise you know me, you know I have no problems stepping away.'

'Aite, fam, I'm sorry, can we just spit bars now, I wanna get on with it,' I tell him. I'm getting nervous. People are watching and he has no idea. But he's not done whining.

'I just think it wouldn't hurt to consider me, and how I feel, every once in a while. Can you do that? Can you do that for me, Growls?' My days, this guy is so annoying. I tell him I'm sorry again and he finally accepts. We continue with the video. He still hasn't noticed the red dot on the screen next to the camera that means people are watching us.

OK, the way this goes is that we take it in turns to beatbox while the other spits bars. We alternate every few lines so that each of us gets time on the mic. Shanks' style is a bit straightforward like Wretch (they share that Caribbean vibe), while my bars are twisty and turny like snakes on a roundabout. Shanks goes first while I drop a beat.

'Yo, Sshhhh, Sshhhanks up here shushing you like we in the library,

Finish other rappers like I'm carefree, I fight scary, my eyes glarey,

Knock down your front door and barge in coz you can't bare me.'

'Yo, Growls taking over, take you downtown like downtown abbey,

My English skills isn't shabby, feds couldn't nab me,

Imporium Armani, Ferrari, night's starry,

Supermarket try bar me, for dropping a jam jari, your bars plain like safari.'

Shanks is still beatboxing but he's tapping his watch because my bars are taking too long. We change over again. Fam, this is fire; we are so easily gonna win that competition.

'Shanks is back spitting litty,

I dominate this rap game just a little bitty,

My bars are gritty, I roll shifty,

Lyrics like a Benz moving nifty, driving past you,

Eyes red like that hamster when it bit me.'

'Yo, Growls is back again,' I jump in.

'I appear as I choose, hard like the beak of a goose,

30

My spirit shape is circle, energy eternal, never run out of duck-duck-juice.'

Mum opens the door and Shanks stops beatboxing so she can come in and collect my laundry. I take this opportunity to quickly look over at the phone. Right now there's 108 people watching us. I hope Tanisha's one of them.

On her way out the door, Mum pauses and turns around. She's holding my underwear in her hand. My heart stops. Before I can react, she marches over like a toy soldier.

'Boy, I told you to wipe your bum properly,' she says, holding up my pants. 'You're not five years old any more.' Mum, no, not like this! The red light is still live on the phone. 'I don't got the time to be wasting on the poopoo of some grown child. Now come put the shopping away.' My stomach is doing a million backflips. There's sweat on my brow, and my head. I reach for the phone before she can do any more damage. 'Boy, leave that phone alone. You don't need it to put shopping away.' Damn.

I leave the phone with Shanks and go help in the kitchen. I'm trying to put the shopping away as fast as I can. The entire time, I'm nervous, I keep dropping stuff. I'm playing the image over and over in my head of her holding my pants and shouting those words. What has she done? I'm gonna have to leave the country and change my identity. It's OK for Shanks, his bars were a bit off, but at least his entire life didn't get finessed dirty for the whole world to see.

31

I finally get back to the room, feeling light-headed and a bit sick. Maybe it's not that bad, I'm sure I can rescue the situation. But when I open the door, Shanks is sitting on the bed, topless, and smelling his fingers. What the actual fresh hell is this?

'Bruv!' I run over to the phone and quickly close the app. The last thing I saw was over 400 viewers. My eyes are stinging and my mouth has gone dry. I turn to Shanks. 'What were you just doing?' My voice is quivering. This guy doesn't know we were live the whole time.

'You were taking long. I was just practising my dance moves to K-pop.'

'But why were you smelling your fingers, fam?' I fall onto the bed, my head in my hands.

'I got sweaty, so I took my shirt off and then I put my fingers in my armpit to check if they smelled like deodorant. I wanted to see if it really is twenty-four-hour protection.' Oh God no, this is a disaster. 'Growls, what's going on? Why you looking at me like that?'

I'm sitting on the bed, I can't move, my life is over. I need to tell him, but I can't believe this is real. I take a deep breath and count to ten twice. And then I do it, I tell Shanks that we were videoing live. We were streaming to the world. He starts to laugh, but it dies out when he sees I'm not JK-ing. He's gone quiet and his mouth is hanging open in shock. He jumps up and looks like he's gonna punch me. This is bad. He starts shouting like, 'What are we gonna do?' and I start shouting like, 'I don't know!' and he's clawing his face and now he's gently banging his head against the wall. It's too intense in here.

Aftermaths

It's Monday morning and I really don't want to go into school. All yesterday evening I was getting messages to my IG, to my Snap, to my phone, from people who saw what happened. None of them were nice. I still can't believe it; my mum literally held up my doo-doo pants and Shanks legit corrupted his own armpit in front of the whole internet. Some people recorded the whole thing with their phones and now the videos are going viral.

It might actually be so peak that I can't do Raptology. The first thing Adrian did when he got home after football was burst into my room and laugh at me. I tried telling him to leave, but he was there for like a whole ten minutes. The older he gets, the worse he is to me. Just coz I don't go football training and I'm not as road as he is (yet), he acts all tough on me, and it's savage.

As I'm putting on my uniform, my hands are shaking when I do the buttons up. Adrian is in sixth form, so he leaves the house half an hour before I do. Before he left he popped his head in my room and told me I'm gonna get roasted like a Sunday turkey. That's actually kinda mad.

When I leave my yard and get on the bus, people are giggling and openly pointing at me, even the Year Sevens. I get off to walk the rest of the way and see a bunch of them turn around. Why they looking at me like I'm a magician's apprentice?

Shanks isn't waiting for me by the school's back gate where we usually meet, so I head inside on my ones. Some kid tries to trip me up in the corridor, but I can't react coz I'm getting it from all angles like Pythagoras' theorem. I preferred it when they ignored me. The worst is when I try to say hello to Tanisha in the form room, and in front of everyone she says, 'Eugh, don't talk to me, Poo-Pants.' I go sit down next to Shanks' empty chair; I don't blame him for not coming in. You know it's peak when my form tutor asks me if everything is alright because he noticed no one wants to sit near me.

After school I call Shanks to check if we cool. He doesn't answer the first two times but he picks up on thrice.

'Bro, I had the maddest day,' I tell him. 'It was so bad that I had to blank Tanisha for her own safety so the others would leave her alone.'

'Yeah.' His voice sounds different to how it usually is. It's bare croaky. 'Today's been kinda wild.' He tells me he's been getting messages non-stop, some from kids at school and lots from random people. Shanks is more active on socials, and he's counted almost fifty messages from people calling him the 'Peckham Armpit Sniffer'. His voice starts to crack.

We both go silent. I wanna say something but I don't know what. I've known this guy since primary school and he never cries. It's hella strange when we hang up the phone, because it's the first time we've ever called each other and not ended up in a good mood.

Shanks doesn't come in the next day either. Again I'm looking over at his empty seat. Not seeing him is like when you leave the house and you left your mobile phone or your heart at home.

Today is worse than yesterday. Anton and Olu are the class bullies, and they've been doing everything they can to make my life miserable. They were throwing paper balls at me in lessons, they spilt their drinks on me during breaktime, and one of them spit on my bag. But it's calm because I always bounce back, like the stock market or a vase.

English class is just before lunch, so I hang back with Mr

Rix because I really can't go back out there again. If I kill enough time, the lunch hall will be emptier, and today I'd prefer to eat alone like a hungry, hungry hippo at a vending machine. If this makes it into my autobiography, I would probably change the names and places and events of this part of the true story.

Mr Rix notices me in the corner practising the electric slide and comes over.

'Listen, Shaun, I can see what's going on and you need to talk to someone. Tell me what happened and maybe we can fix it.' His voice is bare calm and I can see that man's all concerned and that. How do I tell him that my mum held up my doo-doo pants and Shanks did sinister things to his own armpit for the world to see?

'There ain't nothing you can do, sir,' I tell him. 'My life is finished.'

He rolls his eyes; this G isn't taking me seriously. I go to pick up my rucksack but he says something that stops me.

'Accepting help doesn't make you weak, Shaun. In fact, I dare say there is strength of character in asking people to help you out. No one ever has to suffer alone. There is *always* going to be someone who has your back, if you look hard enough for them.'

'No offence, sir, but I don't need anyone to fight my battles. I would be the biggest loser on the planet if I came to you to snake on people.' Swear down, Mr Rix might be

Black, but he's, like, super posh and uses words like 'indeed'. He sighs and sits on the edge of his desk.

'Listen, I know what it's like to be your age, believe it or not. I know it's not "cool" –' he does that "air" quote thing with his "fingers" that I don't really "get" '– to go telling tales, but real life isn't about being cool. You're not a gangster from the Bronx, you're a kid in school with his whole life ahead of him.'

'What do you know? You're posh,' I tell him and pull my bag my over my shoulder, but he's not done.

'Knuckle down, stop daydreaming in class, get your education and give yourself a fighting chance. Prove society wrong. You can be whatever you want to be, you know that, right?'

'I want to be a rapper,' I say.

He rolls his eyes again. 'Why? *Why* do you want to be rapper?'

'Because that gang-gang life is calling me.'

This time he really is done with the convo. He goes back over to his desk and slumps into his chair.

'If any of those kids give you trouble, you know where to find me.'

Mr Rix doesn't know what he's talking about. I ain't grassing on anyone around here. Snitches get stitches. He's not gangster, he's probably gluten-free.

Mum left me and Adrian a potato each for dinner. A *baked* potato, like, that's how I know she don't rate my life. If I get a baked potato, do I not deserve toppings? And if you cut me, do I not bleed. and deserve even more toppings because I'm now bleeding? And I can see an empty box of chicken and chips where Adrian ordered food for himself and not me. He's always overlooking me, like a beautiful sunset above a bridge.

I'm playing FIFA, and there's a grey circle above Shanks' name that shows he's not online. I keep belling his phone, but he ain't picking up. He messaged me to say 'Shaun, this is not a good time. Please respect our privacy.' I don't get it, he never uses my real name, and the way he's writing don't feel right. The words are all boring like an email. It's times like this I go on my 'big feelings' playlist and imagine my future rap career. Sometimes I like when singers have that one hook that I can just vibe to.

6

On My Ones Like a Single Avocado

'Put your shoes on, you're going shopping.' Mum bursts into my room the next afternoon after school and starts ordering me about like a Navy SEAL.

'Please, Mum, I'm playing my game,' I reply. One look at her face and I know I shouldn't have said nothing. I see that vein in her forehead that means she's about to go Super Saiyan level 5.

'If I don't see your shoes on your feet in the next ten seconds, you're going to Tesco's in your socks.'

'Allow me, Mum, I am flesh of your flesh,' I plead, but she's not having it.

Swear down, my mum don't like me, you know. I put my trainers on, the ones with the big hole in the bottom. It tears through my socks when I wear them, which means

40

I can't kneel down coz people will glimpse my bear foot, and I head out into the wild.

I hate going Tesco's. The security guard is bare watching me like Hawkeye, as if I'm gonna take something. This isn't JD Sports, fam, Tesco's don't offer nothing except for dead vegetables like I'm some kinda herb-before, and orange juice that's too cold on my fingers. I get the milk and the bread like Mum wanted, but the things won't scan. Some old lady is tutting because I'm taking so long. I don't know why she's complaining, she ain't got nothing to do except for eat her broken biscuits and quietly breathe in her dusty farts. I don't feel sorry for her, fam, I saw her holding two avocados in her hands, bare feeling them up like a giant afro, but she only bought one. My days, I wish Shanks was here, he knows this Tesco like it's the front of his hand.

On my way home, I take a d-tour past Ilderton Road so I can knock for Shanks, say hello and that. There's no answer at the door, so I call his phone but he doesn't answer that either. I try a few more times before leaving. As I pick up my shopping, I'm sure I see the curtain move in his bedroom. Must have been a pigment of my imagination.

I spend the rest of the afternoon riding my bike around ends. There's no point going home again, Shanks isn't gonna be online anyway. And when I dropped the shopping off, Mum weren't super happy that I bought that lonely avocado that the old lady left behind. My bike is sick

41

though. It's second-hand, which means only one person owned it before me.

I pass Mr Ravi's shop where Mum makes me top up the gas card. She's only given me ten pounds though, and it's usually more than that. Mr Ravi don't care, man's all money. Some sell-out.

Top it up and swing it low, feel the blow,
Chariot of earth and wind carry me home,
Gas for hire, dire need of that energy light like fire,
Biking hits hard, need a Porsche with gas,
Make it from scratch like DreamWorks with that Mad-a-Gas-Card.

I leave the shop and no one's stolen my bike. Mum will be proud of me. She can switch for no reason sometimes, like 'Why did you leave your bike unattended?' or 'This is the real world, magic beans don't exist,' or whatever. I'm cycling the long way round, killing time and going through the backstreets. The playground over there always has an ice-cream van outside it. Mum used to tell me that when the van plays music, that means they've run out of ice cream. If it weren't for Shanks, I would have fully believed her to this day. The playground is also where I got rushed by pigeons because Adrian covered me in birdseed. Mum wasn't even mad, she just laughed at us. That was time ago though, we don't really kick it like that any more. On the left, you can see the empty car park where all the mandem on the block would have water fights in the summer. Water fights ain't fun by yourself, it's just me pouring a bottle over myself and running away. That wall with all the graffiti on it is where we'd gather at the end of a long day. Adrian used to let me chill with him and his friends when Shanks was on holiday. But then they all got old and started leaving me behind, and the kids on the estate assumed I was weird because I would shout at pigeons who got too brave.

When I get home I go straight to my room and put my headphones on. I like it when the flow's hard and the beat has trumpets and stuff in it. I know Adrian likes Ghetts because his wordplay is wild, but I think Dave has better music.

Mum is watching her series in the living room before she goes to work, and it sounds like Adrian is in the kitchen. I flop down on the bed and open my messages. I really want to chat to Shanks, tell him about my day and that, but this guy been ghosting like the spirit of Mufasa, the one true king of the pride lands. I wanna tell him that I went to the playground and sat on our see-saw, but it was really boring without another person. I wanna tell him that I saw the guy at the bus stop that always wears a long coat, the one who looks like he's had a troubled past.

I look at my PlayStation. There's no point in even turning it on, I know Shanks ain't gonna be there. All the texts on my phone are from me to Shanks, and I'm finally starting to get the message. OMG, did I just use a metaphor? Can't lie, being without him like this reminds me of when Mum got Adrian a phone but not me. I was so upset that in the end she gave me a yogurt pot with a string attached to it. You're supposed to talk into it, and the person holding the other side can hear you like it's a phone. Bruh, there wasn't even another yogurt pot on the other end.

These days are all blurring into one like binge-watching. It's been almost a week since we did the armpit-pants video, but I ain't really seen Shanks in all that time. He came into school with his mum yesterday morning; I saw them walking towards the office where the headteacher lives. Mrs Shanks was bare frowning, proper serious, and he was just following her, staring at the ground with his hands in his pockets and not making eye contact. It was peak because some kids were shouting stuff at him like, 'What is this wasteman doing back?' and I'm pretty sure he heard because he flinched. I wanted to go running over, tell them all to allow it, but I knew if I did it would just make things worse. Someone even tried to throw an empty can at him, but they stopped when his mum gave them the same look she gives me when I finish all the orange juice in her house. Don't mess with them Caribbean mums, boy, they will finish you like a bottomless brunch.

Twenty minutes later I saw her drag him out of the office

and start heading to the car. This time I panicked and ran after them, shouting his name. What if he didn't come back? His mum looked angrier than a dog trainer who's been duped by a bunch of cats in disguise. I didn't care if people were watching. But Shanks and his mum didn't stop. Then as she started the engine, he looked up and saw me running towards them. He looked proper excited, tapping his mum on the shoulder and pointing at me. His mouth was moving like he was saying something, but she shook her head, and he slumped back into his chair. In the end she started driving away and he just pressed his hand up against the window to say goodbye.

Life is hard without him, for real. I'm really starting to miss him. Like, it's Friday afternoon right now, and we would always go to the 99p shop and see how many cans of Coke we could get for a pound. But that grey circle is still next to Shanks' name on FIFA. Usually we'd play all night. I would win proper easily, like Manchester City vs a team of children who have giant broccoli stems instead of legs. That image is shocking – those kids would be falling over everywhere.

I use the spare time to write lyrics, *although the cynics would question the physics of my lyrics and try mimic the timid hymns that I finish*. Bars. Poetic.

Lay Miserables

It's Sunday afternoon and I'm practising kick-ups in the football cage alone. There's a bunch of people playing a match, but I don't wanna join in because it would be unfair for the other team. Last time I played football, I did a literal bicycle kick and everyone was like, 'Oh my gosh, that was amazing!' and, 'You're not allowed to ride that in here,' and, 'What are you doing, this is a basketball match.' I feel my phone vibrating, and when I answer, Mum's voice sounds a little worried.

'Shaun, it's your friend, Shanks.'

'No, it's not, it's my mum. I can hear your voice, and your name flashed up on my phone.'

'No, Shaun, you don't understand.' She doesn't sound angry for once. 'I got a call from his mum. You need to come home.' Skeen. How is this woman gonna summon me home like a Wizard of Oz? Swear down, she can wait, fam. But just in case it's important, I hurry back.

When I come through the front door, she's sitting at the kitchen table looking serious. What have I done now? I'm racking my brains for, like, two seconds, but I can't think of anything.

'Sit down,' she says. I slowly pull up a chair opposite her. The trick is not to break eye contact. She can hear Adrian shuffling around, so she gets up to close the door and sits down again. 'Shanks isn't doing too good. He's in hospital.'

I jump straight out of my chair.

'What? Did he fall over? Is it bad? We need to go see him.' I'm being bare frantic. Oh my God I hope he's OK. It must be serious if my mum is sitting here at the table talking to me like she's Alan Sugar. 'Mum, we have to go see him, you have to take me.' Why is she not moving? Why is she not putting her coat on right now to take me to him? 'Mum?'

'We can't see him, not just yet. He won't be around for a while.' What the hell does that mean?

'Mum, please. I have to see him, when can we go?'

She just shakes her head. 'You can't see him right now. Look, son, his mum told me he's been tired, stressed, and that's made him unwell. We need to wait and see the situation, but right now he's not allowed visitors.' My insides are going cold.

'Mum . . .' I start to feel water in my eyes. 'Mum, please. Please don't do this to me. I'm sorry for all the things that I've done, and I promise I'll try to do better. But you have to take me to see Shanks.'

I get half hopeful when she stands up, but she's just going to work.

'Shaun, my hands are tied on this one. We have to respect their wishes.' Her hand hesitates over the door handle for a split second, her eyes all wide. She looks like she's about to turn around and say something else, but then she frowns, straightens up and walks out.

I can't believe Shanks is in hospital. What if he's waiting for me and I'm not there?

I have to curl up into a ball. I'm just a ball, lying in the dark on the carpet next to my bed. I scroll on my phone to find a song, but I don't want to listen to any of them. In the end I dash my phone onto a pile of clothes on the floor. The light switch is so far away. Far, far away, just like the galaxy. Me and Shanks saw that film in the cinema. He paid for my ticket. I should have paid. I should have always paid. That poo video that ruined us doesn't feel important any more, the only thing that matters is that my best friend gets better. When he's better, we're gonna kick ball in the football cage, ride our bikes and eat hot wings in our favourite spot up on Telegraph Hill. But for now I'll stay curled in a ball on the floor and wait for him to get better.

* * *

School the next day is really strange. I feel like I'm missing part of body, like my ghoul bladder or my sarcophagus. Ever since his mum came in last week and drove him away, people been chatting about what could've happened. When he's not in school again today, I think they might have clocked that he ain't coming back any time soon. When I walk into the form room everyone's whispering but for once no one is mocking it. The teachers are being bare kind to me, like I'm the one who's sick.

It gets worse when my form tutor asks me to hang back before first lesson. He thinks it's a good idea for me to chat to someone who ain't a teacher, about anything that's troubling me. It doesn't sound like I have a choice, so I just stay silent, like the time I hid in the wrong cupboard at a surprise party. The school counsellor's name is Karen, and apparently I can say anything I want to her in confidence. I've got an appointment to see her later this week. Allow my life.

After lunch, Tanisha breaks off from her galdem and comes over to me outside the hall. After she dropped me like a boiled potato, she's moving suspect by approaching me in the open planes. Tanisha says that she heard about Shanks, and asks if the rumours are true. I don't know what she's talking about because there are so many rumours in the

49

world; I once heard that Trinidad and Tobago are the same place. She's saying that there's a rumour going round that Shanks isn't coming in because he's in hospital, and other people are saying that his mum shipped him to Jamaica.

And, like, it's calm that she's back on it with me, and blatantly begging for an invite to the next Princess Buttercup film, but right now I just wanna hide in Mr Rix's room. He's been acting kind of safe this last week. He's been letting me sit in his class at break and lunch and he doesn't chat the most, he just eats and marks homework and scrolls on his phone. He does talk to me sometimes, about the future and that, and even tells me stuff about English that helps with my lyrics. Other times he puts classical music on and I pretend like it's not a proper vibe, even though I'm low-key enjoying it.

But I know that the minute I leave Mr Rix's room, a tiger wave of emotions will hit me.

It's the last lesson of the afternoon and Ms Marapova, my maths teacher, is stressing out at me. She's always giving me and Shanks detention for rapping in class. It's not my fault that I already know all the numbers. I hate walking into a lesson and not seeing him there; this one hurts extra hard because we'd always do our detentions together.

When Ms Marapova calls my name out for the register to see if I'm here, she's looking right at me. But I can't do it any more, if Shanks isn't here then I don't wanna be either. She can keep calling like a mamma penguin for its baby, but I don't feel the need to respond. I put my head down on the desk and try to fast-forward the lesson. She calls my name again and I still don't say anything. I'm worried that if I try to say anything, I'm going to start crying and make a fool out of myself in front of everyone. Even when I open my mouth to reply, the bubble in my chest gets stuck and starts turning into needles. I can't. She calls my name one more time, but I stay silent. Ms Marapova's had enough. She tells me to go for a walk, clear my head a little, and come back when I'm ready. This feels like a trap, and I ain't talking about the music. But if she calls my mum, I ain't even nervy. Mum doesn't answer calls from unknown numbers, she knows that the FBI and the Mazda MI5 are tryna eavesdrop on conversations.

My eyes are stinging as I leave the room. I kick a chair on the way out and everyone gasps. Rule one of being a G on road, never let them see you cry.

As soon as I get back from school, Mum's all over me like a rash, the kind that you get when you use Dettol wipes instead of toilet paper. Ms Marapova must have called to snitch on me already, like some snaky don in Nike gloves. She says she's sick of me moping around the house and acting up at school. She says it's not what Shanks would

51

want, and I tell her that she don't know what Shanks would want. Then my eyes start leaking from the kettle steam. Can't lie, I do wish I had someone to talk to about this stuff. Maybe the school counsellor knows someone . . .

I'm chilling with Mr Rix the next day, and he's already heard about what happened in maths class. *Marapova got that spread, spread, spread like butter on bread.* The look on his face makes me feel proper guilty. He understands when I explain it to him, but he's happy that I'll be doing the counselling, and I guess he's pretty smart.

This guy's a teacher with class,
Classy music, man gives me a pass,
Ain't no quick fix,
Ain't no fit bits, unfit to chill outside of here with Mr Rix.
Drop a beat, eat, sleep, learn, gain, grain but none that dry wheat,
Don't ever repeat the weak beat like dry Weetabix.

Swear down, Mr Rix is the calmest teacher, not like some of the others.

'Sir, I don't like Ms Marapova talking about me, using my name for clout. If she wants followers, she should make a video on TikTok where she line-dances in front of the I-Fall Tower.' Mr Rix closes his eyes tight and shakes his head. I might have gone too far with that one.

'I assure you, she was not gossiping, nor will she *ever* feel the need to line-dance in front of historical monuments in the manner you suggested.' He lets out a long sigh. 'Shaun, I'm not going to comment on Ms Marapova, that's not my place. But as your teacher, I am going to need you to be better.' He looks over at the door and then back at me. 'Listen, for kids who are into rap music and talk the way you do, the world out there can be extremely unforgiving.' He stops for a second. 'Look at what's happening all around the globe.' I think I know what he's talking about, because I seen some stuff on TikTok, but I tell him all that's in America. This ain't the same.

'It's not just in America. Unfortunately, when you have a certain background, the world tends to look at you a little differently. You're going to come up against employers, educators, people in the street, airline security, the whole lot. I'm not saying everyone will think less of you, I'm just letting you know that it's never a surprise when they do.'

'Even you? But you're posh.'

'Yes, but you think the way I talk stops people judging me when I walk into a room? You think if I use big words that years of bigotry vanish into thin air? People judge others based on what they see, and rarely what they know.'

I try to make sense of it all. 'Sir? What happens if things don't change?'

'Accept the things that you can't change, like the past, and make sure that you work towards a better future. Remember, Shaun, change can only happen if we *believe* that change can happen. And I believe that you can be a true example that there's infinitely more to people than meets the eye.'

8

In My Feelings Like R'n'B

It's proper peak on Wednesday morning because everyone stares at me when the counsellor interrupts our maths class to take me to our session. I don't look anyone in the eye as I drag my bag across the classroom floor and follow her out into the corridor.

The counsellor's office is in one of the staff rooms. The ceiling has a stain on it like in my derelict bedroom, and there's nothing here except a few sofas and a water machine. Me and Shanks tried to steal a water machine once, but we just knocked it over by accident and ran away. That day was kinda lit. I got chased by a dog and fell in a lake, so Shanks bought me Iceland cheesecake to cheer me up. This counsellor's not going to buy me a cheesecake though.

Karen looks like she sings to her aloe vera plants. She's

wearing *two* silky scarves, even though we're inside. She invites me to sit on the sofa; it's kinda comfy, and I guess this is why people are always saying 'sofa so good'. I know from the films you're supposed to lie on a couch and cry about feelings while the therapist doodles in their notepad. I don't know if I should be sitting or lying down. I try kneeling, but she's looking at me weird, so I slowly slide onto my side like Mum's Lionel Ritchie album cover. I feel like a mermaid.

'You can just sit how you would on a regular chair.' A'ite, cool. 'Growls, is it? Tell me more about yourself.'

'I eat ham rolls for breakfast.' She raises her eyebrows. Why is her face so kind? She's too happy for a weekday morning. I don't like it.

'And why do people call you Growls?'

'Because I'm a G on road. Because I been known to be "tiger-like" when I spit bars. What other things you wanna know?' Yo, this lady's not phased at all. She tells me that this is a safe space, which I guess is calm because it means there's no fire hazards or sharp objects.

'I think it's important for you to know that I'm not here to intrude, or to "fix" anything.' Karen says. 'Nothing you say to me goes beyond these four walls if you don't want it to, just think of me as someone completely impartial that you can talk to.'

'If everything I say stays in this room, then why do you have a notepad?'

She tells me it's a good question and that she sometimes makes notes for her own benefit, to document any dates or themes we chat about, and I can just ignore them. Fam, last time I ignored a doctor's notes, I started brushing my teeth with foot cream.

'I know how tough it is to open up to a stranger, and I know you don't know me yet, but let me first say, you shouldn't think of me as a teacher.' When she says that, I feel my whole body get less tense. Maybe she's kinda legit. 'Listen, can I be sincere with you right now?' She leans in. 'And if you still don't feel like talking then we can sit in silence for the next forty-five minutes.'

OK, I'm proper curious now.

'My only task for today is to have an open and honest conversation with you. If we do that, I walk away happy, you walk away happy, and we'll both be stuffing our faces in the canteen at breaktime before we know it. Deal?'

OK, she's not tryna finesse me. She seems legit, and she's not chatting down to me.

'Deal.' I tell her. She smiles at me and then starts asking random questions like 'What's your favourite TV show?' and that kind of stuff. Can't lie, I do miss chatting about this kinda stuff with Shanks. When I let that slip to Karen, the mood starts changing a bit.

'Your friend Shanks, can you tell me a little bit about him?'

'He's aite.' She waits for me to say something else. It's getting awkward, and I can feel my body tensing up again. Just talking about him, I'm imagining Shanks in a hospital bed while I'm here on this nice couch.

Karen looks at her notes. 'I understand you two are close?'

'Close? Nah, London Bridge and Tower Bridge are close, Shanks is my brother.'

'Can you elaborate? As in, what kind of things do you get up to?' Karen's doing prayer hands emoji to her mouth right now.

I find myself replying without even thinking about it. 'Well, he isn't just my OG, he's the part of me that isn't trapped in these ends. He makes me stand up on the train when old women with shopping need to sit down. He's like the older brother to me that Adrian could never be #metaphor.' I tell Karen about all the times we be chilling at Shanks' house, playing FIFA and eating chicken and chips. Or how we'd spend whole afternoons riding our bikes down Glenn Close, where we'd sit on the wall and read fortune cookies to each other. I tell her about how he winged it for me when I got Tanisha's number. I even tell her about the video scandal, about how peak it was for him online. And now he's in hospital and I don't even know if he's OK. Fam, this is getting heavy.

Karen frowns and looks at her notes again. Then she looks up at me. 'It sounds like you guys have been through a lot together. And I can see how it can be very upsetting, but I can assure you that Shanks is exactly where he needs to be right now,' she says, 'and that he is being looked after by the right people.'

Straight up, I feel a microwave of relief. My head feels light, like I might float to the ceiling.

'You must be happy with that news?'

'Yeah, of course.' I think I'm having an allergic reaction to the spores in the room because my eyes are leaking.

'And do you think you can tell me why?'

'I don't know.' I'm wiping the tears from cheeks. 'Because I didn't want him to be sick or in pain or nothing. He doesn't deserve that.' Now that I know he's going to be OK, I don't have to worry so much about not ever seeing him again. I've been so scared for him these last few days. Wow, I've been *so* scared. I just never thought about it like that.

'Everybody gets scared at some point. Everyone,' Karen says. 'Adults, schoolkids, all your favourite superheroes, everyone. I believe that voicing your fears gives you power over them, it gives them nowhere to hide.'

'For real?' I don't wanna be scared no more.

'Of course! Let's give it a go. What are you afraid of? What kinds of things keep you up at night?'

'Adrian playing loud music.' I think she thinks that I'm joking. I don't know why everyone always thinks I'm joking. I wish I could talk to someone about that. I'm thinking about other things that scare me, there's probably one or two. 'Being ignored, I guess.' She nods, and it feels really good that Karen's listening. It proper makes me want to continue. 'Loud noises scare me too. And voodoo magic, like curses and stuff. The thought of slipping in the bath and busting my head on the tap. Paper hats, that's another one that doesn't make sense. How is it flat paper one minute, and then it's a 3D hat, like, I don't get the science. Some cats, but only when they're face height, like, sat on a wall or something. Or, like, some mornings I wake up and I'm scared we're gonna run out of hot water again; last week I had to eat a very crunchy Pot Noodle. Oh, and girls with long nails. Like, how do you wipe after the toilet?'

Karen leans back in her chair and breathes out. 'OK. Let's . . . You said something fascinating that I'd like to explore. You said you're scared of being ignored.' She looks at me and smiles.

I can't help it, I can feel my face fighting it, but I think I'm smiling back. 'Yeah, I guess.'

'How does it feel, not currently having someone you can confide in?'

When I deep it, it's actually kinda lonely, still. Not seeing Shanks ain't the worst, like he goes on holiday sometimes and we don't see each other, which is fine, but I would always tell him about my day. Now that he's not online, I don't have no one else to say stuff to. The other kids at school just blank me like the back of a treasure map, Mum's always at work, and me and Adrian don't chat like that. I guess I can talk to Mr Rix about some stuff, but he's a teacher so it doesn't count. I tell Karen that it feels like I got nobody to turn to, forever alone and that.

She closes her eyes and nods.

Yo, I have to be real with it, big man ting.

'I'm just tired of drawing fake lips on my hand with my mum's lipstick and kissing my thumb.' She opens her eyes. 'Sometimes, when I'm feeling delicate, I don't even use tongue, I just lightly kiss it like the Pope's ring.' Karen opens her mouth like she's about to say something, but closes it again.

She takes a deep breath. 'You're not alone, Growls. Your feelings of isolation are totally valid, but there's always people you can talk to, including me, OK?' I nod. 'Just like we did when you listed your fears, talking about things that scare and upset you are the first step to conquering them. You don't have to keep things bottled up.'

I'm actually kinda relieved when she tells me to take a business card with a number I can reach her on. I guess if I'm proper desperate, I know I can call and have a conversation with someone. But, like, proper desperate.

'Tell me, Growls, how do you feel right now? Having opened up. That wasn't that bad, was it?' She does a little laugh. 'At least not as boring as it would've been if we sat in silence for forty-five minutes.' Yo, how she laughing at her own dead joke like it banged?

You know what, I don't mind, she's cool. And she's right, wow, I do feel much lighter. And weirdly a lot freer.

When it's time for me to leave, I almost don't wanna go. I didn't think I'd enjoy this so much, but I guess anything is possible. Except for time travel, cloning sheep and an Elvis Presley reunion tour.

I put my coat on but there's one more question I have to ask.

'Karen?'

'Yes, Growls.'

'The other day in my maths class I was moving kinda wild. I even kicked a chair and that on my way out. Like, I know I make bad decisions sometimes,' I tell her, 'I just, I kinda need to know if I'm a bad guy or not.'

She thinks about it for a sec. 'If you're *worried* about being a bad guy, to use your terminology, I think it proves that you're not one.'

Lynx Africa ((oz Romance Ain't Dead)

You know what, I think everything's gonna be alright. Karen is right. As the next week goes by and the weather gets a bit warmer, I'm getting more and more excited for when I might see Shanks again. We're gonna go back to Mr Ravi's corner shop and eat sweets. I been saving up my lunch money to spend on Shanks when he comes back. We're gonna play end-to-end in the cage and drink Ribena in our favourite spot overlooking the London lights.

Today I can smell cooking and barbecues outside, one of the signs that summer's on its way, and it puts a big smile on my face. I think of Nigerian jollof rice and paper plates that go all greasy on the underside, so you have to wipe your fingers on your jeans when nobody's looking. But good moods are like pet goldfish when you feed them

Diet Coke, they never last very long. Mum's just as evil as ever. It's Saturday and she's still sending me on errands and that. Real gangsters don't go round doing their mother's bidding. She needs to put some respect on my name.

Right now, she's making me bring some grilled chicken and rice to her friend Jackie, who lives in the block across the road. I tried to say no, but my mum just can't accept that I'm a big man on road. When she sends us to do stuff like this, me and Adrian play a game of 'rock paper punch' to decide who goes. Its like 'rock paper scissors' except it hurts and I never win. This one time we played, I almost cried into my sleeve and he told me to toughen up. He said I need to be stronger out in the world.

Bruv, my mum makes the tastiest food for the neighbours but gets vexed whenever we ask for some. For real, I once saw her wrap some roasted stuffed peppers in fifty layers of cling film while I just watched and ate a cornflake sandwich.

On my way home from Jackie's, I spot some kids playing on their balcony above me. Even though kids at school have stopped cussing at me, I still get recognised in the ends for that video. Swear down, I can't walk nowhere. People keep pointing at me in the street and laughing like 'Hey, is that him? Is that the kid from the video?' I try to walk past quickly with my head down, but one of the youngers spots me and they start shouting stuff. Even through my headphones I hear them calling, 'Hey, look, it's him, it's poo-pants boy'. I wanna respond, but I know the loud one has an older brother. If there's beef and the brother comes for me, I would have no choice but to use lethal force, and that is something I will not do. My sashimi training has taught me better than that. It's better that I just go home and practise my street-dance moves.

When I get home, it's still early and I don't want to stay indoors all day. Adrian left his basketball by the front door, so I might borrow it and shoot some hoops. I think of inviting him, but Adrian's no fun any more. He used to be when we were younger, but now he's always shouting and tryna throw darts at me.

When I get there, the basketball cage is empty. There's three different blocks that look down on the cage, so maybe someone will come down and join me. Actually, when I deep it, it's probably best that they don't come out. They'd just say some next stuff about my pants that isn't true. I don't care because I'm just here to practise anyway. By the time Shanks comes back, I'll be greater than that French basketball player, Le Bron James. I'll only score three-point shots until I reach one hundred, Shanks is gonna love it.

I walk out into the middle of the cage, bouncing the ball as I move. The trick is to not accidentally bounce it onto your foot and make it roll away from you, because then you have to chase it and look around quickly to make sure nobody saw. You also can't hold the ball and run with it, otherwise people on your team get vexed and chase you out the cage.

I set my phone to video and put it on the floor to record my greatness. I'm trying to prop it up on a water bottle I found, but it keeps slipping down again. See, this is why I don't drink water. In the end, I take off my shoe and prop the phone up on that instead, Mamma didn't raise no fool. It's a good thing I'm wearing both socks today.

With the phone recording, I step onto the court and start doing some mad trick shots. The first one is where I cover my eyes and shoot the ball. I think it went in, but I can't tell because I can't see. The next one I do is where I face away from the hoop and throw the ball over my shoulder. Can't lie, I have to do it four or five times to get my technique perfect, although they probably all went in because I have good karma and foot placement. Now I'm gonna try a through-the-legs dribble shot. I get most of it right, but I'm doing too much with the dribble. I wipe my mouth and get back into view of the video.

Someone is walking past, they might wanna play, but then I spot it's just some old man walking his dog.

I'm getting bored of trick shots, it's not as fun without Shanks screaming every time I get one in the hoop. I start doing free throws instead, the trick is to let fly and hope for the best.

'Wow, you haven't made a single shot.' There's a girl in

the cage standing behind me, and one of us screamed in fear because I didn't hear her come in. She has red hair and Converse, and she does not look impressed. It's funny, she's kinda beautiful, but in a different way to Tanisha. Her nail varnish is chipped, like she's active, but her hands look soft. And her eyes are bare green, like one of them fake plants that you don't have to water. She looks nice. But why she @ing my skills though?

'What you talking about? Of course I made a shot,' I tell her. 'You just didn't see it.'

'I've been sat on that bench for half an hour, and you haven't got the ball in the hoop once. You need to bend your knees more and release the ball as you're springing up. And it helps if you're wearing both shoes.' Bruh, how is this girl gonna tell me how many shoes I need to wear?

'If you know anything about basketball, you'll know that Le Bron sometimes wears one shoe.'

'No, he doesn't.' She looks confused.

'Well ...' I have to think about it for a sec. 'After he puts his first shoe on, he's only wearing one shoe until he puts the second one on. Hah, gottem.' I do a quick dab and she looks like she's about to laugh. Ain't no one can test me on my basketball knowledge.

'Well, while I'm here, maybe we can do a one v. one?' She picks up the ball and bounces it a couple times. 'Who knows, you might learn a thing or two.' She sticks out her tongue, bare playful and that. Well, joke's on her, I already know at least two things.

We start a game up to ten. I let her go first because she was holding the ball and I don't have a choice.

Yo, she's not bad. She's a bit smaller than me but she gets past my block like a ghost in the wind. She's pretty good at jump shots too. I lose track of the score after 5–0, but it's not about winning or losing. This is actually calm, it's been a while since I got to do anything with someone. I don't know if she's going easy on me or if I'm playing bad because I'm still only wearing one shoe, but either way we carry on.

After a while I'm getting too thirsty. It's hot and there's no shade in the cage and my mouth is going dry. I have to go home and get some water before I pass out. I don't really know how to say goodbye to the girl, so I do a cool fist bump and hope she remembers this magical afternoon forever.

When I leave the cage, I see that the kids who were shouting at me from the balcony are still there, so I have to hurry past before they notice me again and start yelling stuff. Someone taps me on the shoulder.

'Excuse me.'

'I do not have poo-pants!' I shout, turning around. But it's just the redhead girl from the cage. She's bare baffled.

'Oh. OK. No, it's just that I think you dropped something while we were playing.' She holds up my pineapple-passion lip balm that must have fallen out my pocket.

'Oh. Thanks.' This is kinda awkward, I normally carry cherry blossom.

She doesn't leave though.

'Why did you say that thing before?'

'What thing?'

'That thing about your pants.'

'Stop making things up, I didn't say nothing.' She doesn't look like she believes me, but she properly introduces herself. Her name's Shevon and she lives near the playground. I tell her I've never seen her around ends before, and she just shrugs and says she doesn't leave the house much during the day. I don't know how, but we end up walking together.

'How are you so good at basketball?' I ask her.

'I used to play netball,' she shrugs. 'What, why are you smirking?'

'Netball's just a rubbish version of basketball, they don't even have it in the Winter Olympics.'

'Well, they don't have basketball either,' she says. I guess that's fairy nuff.

When I ask her what school she goes to, she tells me the maddest thing. She's homeschooled.

'Does that mean you're dumb, if you only get home-schooled? Like all your lessons are about your home and you don't learn nothing else?' Maybe I could teach her about the world.

'Um, homeschooled just means I'm taught at home. I'm not taught *about* my home. That would be pointless.'

'Oh yeah? Would it be pointless to know where the escape routes are in the event of a fire? Or how long a month of heating costs in the winter?' Wow. That all seems like useful information. Now I wanna be homeschooled.

It's wild that she only lives by the playground, it's just three minutes from my yard. My mum would tell me that if I go to that playground alone, a stranger would kidnap me in his ice-cream van and feed me to wolves. I ask Shevon if she knows any ice-cream-van kidnappers.

'No. That's a weird thing to ask.'

'Cool,' I reply. I guess she has a point. 'Hey, Shevon, have you ever filmed yourself doing the moonwalk and then played it in reverse so it looks like you're walking forward?'

'I can't say I have, no. I guess I could just film myself walking forward. But why would I do that?' Geez, this girl's got an answer for everything. She looks me up and down. 'You don't have many friends, do you?'

'Skeen. I got lots of friends. A lot of them are online, and my boy Shanks is also my MC partner, but he ain't about because he's ill,' I tell her. 'Where are all *your* friends?' I ask her, see how she likes it.

'I don't have any either. I'm homeschooled, remember?' Oh. Shevon's real with it, I like that. I tell her that we can be friends and I only live up the road.

70

'Yo, what's your number? Maybe we can hang out sometimes or whatever,' I ask her.

'I don't have a phone,' she says. I'm waiting for the punchline. There is no punchline. She's being serious.

'You don't have a phone? But how do you Snap? How do you post stories? Oh my days, how do you scroll?' Yo, this is too much madness. Seriously, this is the weirdest thing I've ever heard. Geez, and I thought *my* mum was bad. How can someone our age not have a phone? Phone is life. Phone is love. 'How do I hit you up then?'

'I live at number 23, you can just knock for me.'

'Skeen. What am I – a postman?'

'Well, how do you think people met up before phones were invented?'

'I don't know. But at least I can google it on my phone.'

'So without a phone you don't know anything?' She pokes her tongue out again to mock me. It makes my stomach do a little backflip and I get flustered. Her smile is like a taste-the-rainbow with the bowl of Skittles at the end of it. But then she looks at her watch and lets out a little scream. Apparently, she's late and has to hurry home to make dinner. I think she means she has to *eat* dinner.

When she turns to go, I ask if we can meet up again because she seems like she needs a friend. She tells me to knock for her on Monday at around 4 p.m. and we can hang out. I watch her get further and further away until she turns the corner and disappears.

When I get home, Mum's already left for work. Adrian's probably out, but I call around the flat just to make sure. I know he's not asleep, because I can't hear him snoring. He sounds like a buffalo drowning in milkshake.

You know what, I'm not even gonna go straight to my room. Instead I eat a couple Scotch eggs and chill in the kitchen, I never do that. I'm happily munching them down, thinking about all the stuff that's happened this the last week. With the therapy with Karen and then meeting Shevon and that, I've got multiple stories, just like a car park.

I know he won't answer, but I text Shanks about my day. I don't mind being alone today, it's not that deep, but I do kinda wish Mum was here so I could ask for an update, see if she's heard any more from Shanks' mum. I tell him all about how I met a girl whose number I would have got, but she don't have a phone, and she lives local like Co-op.

When I wake up the next morning, I realise it's the first time in ages that I've actually fallen asleep that easily.

Postman Pat on the Back

School on Monday goes by real quick. I'm knocking for Shevon on the way home, and when the bell goes at 3.30 pm. I'm the first one out the door. It would be decent if Shanks was with us, maybe not the first few times but later, once Shevon's acclimatised to our friendship. I can picture us all hanging out as a batch, and in the words of Albert Eye-Stein: 'If you can dream it, you can do it.' I saw that on Instagram.

I get to number 23 and the curtains are closed. I guess that makes sense because the sun is out, and some people get sunburned. The flowers in the pot outside the doorway are dried out, and the gate creaked so loudly that I don't even think Shevon needs a doorbell. She opens the door and hurries out before I have time to knock.

'I need to be back at six, so I'm counting on you to make this fun,' she says.

She's counting on me? No one's ever done that. The only thing I can count on is a calculator, and even then I only use it to spell fun words. Eight million eight thousand one hundred and thirty-five, that's all I'm saying.

Shevon suggested Costa. I've never been inside, but she says that they do nice cookies and I ask her if it's free.

'Of course not. Why would it be free?' she says.

'Because it wouldn't Costa thing,' I say back to her.

'That's so silly,' she laughs.

For real though, I only got four pounds on me, that's my lunch money that I didn't spend today, just in case we went Chicken Cottage and I could get us four wings and chips. Luckily Shevon has her own funds that she keeps in an actual purse like an adult, none of this loose change clinking around like Tinkerbell, you feel me?

The Costa on our high street is pretty big, it has couches everywhere, and people are working on their laptops, and mums and their kids are sitting around chatting. It's a bit of a wholesome vibe, can't lie.

Shevon gets a chocolate muffin and I get a croissant that's shaped like a prawn in a Chinese takeaway and bare flaky like it's made from dried leaves. It bangs though. When we sit down, she starts picking the muffin apart with her hands. Her red hair looks cool on her pale skin, she's like a manga character. Just being next to her, my chest is hammering way too fast and I wanna hold her hand and do a fun dance. I can't stop staring. She catches me smiling as I watch her and we both look away.

'How comes you need to be back at six?' I ask. She doesn't respond straight away, then just says she doesn't wanna talk about it, which I completely understand. I ask her why she doesn't wanna talk about it.

'It's just private. Can we talk about something else?' she says, folding her arms.

I think I've upset her so I change the subject real quick. 'OK, I got one. We can play "would you rather",' I tell her.

She agrees and immediately starts thinking of what to ask. Shevon frowns when she thinks, she's proper smart like one of those genius test-tube babies who was born in a science lab.

'You said you're part of a rap duo.'

'Yeah, MC Squared.' I fold my arms and go to do my back-to-back pose with Shanks, but he's not here so it just feels silly.

'So would you rather be a professional basketball player or a professional rapper?'

'Rapper.' That one was easy, I don't even have to think about it. 'Even though I'm a seven out of nine at basketball, rapping is my true passionfruit. *I spit bars in the bakery, no bun intended, eleven eggs didn't break but one in ten did, I was running and walking before feet were invented.*'

Shevon's grinning and clapping, saying that was actually quite good. Can't lie, I'm kinda gassed. She has hobbies as well; she loves painting and drawing and wants to open a gallery some day. I ain't into that art stuff, but I kinda like that she likes it.

OK, it's my turn.

'Would you rather have one eye, or be forced to raise a family of baby rats for the rest of your life but they never grow old?' She laughs like I made a joke, so I guess I have to laugh along too.

'That's so random! You're supposed to say something like, "Would you rather have chips or nuggets?" Yours was just strange.'

'How is it strange? Just answer the question, fam.'

'OK, so my choices are basically between being a Cyclops or a surrogate mother to rodents . . .' she says.

After a sec I tell her that, if it helps, she can be a two-eyed Cyclops. 'A two-eyed Cyclops? So just a normal human being then. I choose that.'

'No, your eyes would be one on top of the other. It'd look really weird, but I guess it's handy for seeing over things.' This is kinda fun.

'Well, in that case I choose the rats.' She's smiling and it makes me tingly like mint shower gel but on the inside. She gives me her scenario. 'Would you rather have dinner with Queen Victoria or your great-great grandad?'

'Hah, that's a trick question,' I answer. 'They're both dead so neither of them would be able to eat anything.' She looks baffled and I tell her it's my turn again.

'Erm, no, it's not your turn. Obviously I meant for them to be alive in this hypothetical. Why would I ask you to choose between two corpses to have dinner with?'

'I don't know, bruh, because you're bad at the game? Even if they were both alive, I didn't know my great-great grandad, and Queen Victoria was bare boring. All she did was name a train station after herself and she wasn't even able to stop World War Two.'

'That's because she died about forty years before it started.'

'Or so she says.' You can't test my history knowledge, I been clued up. This one time, I asked my mum if she did history at school. When she said yes, I was confused and asked her what they talked about because nothing had happened yet.

'OK, I got a good one. Would you rather have curtains for arms or a dead mum?'

Immediately Shevon switches and looks like I just threw a drink in her face. 'That's not even funny.' She crushes the piece of muffin she's holding in her hand. 'I love my mum, and I would never, ever want her to die. You know what, I don't wanna play this dumb game any more.' She goes back to eating her muffin.

Fam, I don't know what to talk about any more, I keep

saying the wrong things. The more I try to impress her, the worse this is going. Maybe I just need to calm down, I shouldn't be thinking so hard, I should just say the first thing that pops into my head.

'Have you ever tried to put your foot behind your head and accidentally smelt the underside of your own knee?'

Shevon looks up again, giving me some major side-eye with her mouth half open so I can see chocolate inside.

'No.' We sit in silence for a bit and then she stands up to leave, pushing the chair back with her legs. It's not even five o'clock, we still have a whole hour. My days, this is like Tanisha all over again.

'Wait, before you go, I wanted to give you something,' I tell her. I might not get another chance. She pauses and raises one eyebrow like The Rock. I reach into my pocket and pull out a spare pineapple-passion lip balm, barely used. 'It's how we became friends and I thought it would be cool if we both have one, like being in a club or something. And I'm sorry about the thing that I said before, I wasn't trying to make you sad.' I hold out the lip balm and she kinda smiles. I want her to use some now because her lips are a bit dry, but I decide not to tell her that. Her finger touches mine as she takes it, and my face has to concentrate on not getting embarrassed.

'OK, fine, I can stay a little longer.' She sits down opposite me again. We spend some time playing eye-spy and I point out that if she was a two-eyed Cyclops, the game would be called eye-eye spy. She asks me if I have any brothers or sisters, and I tell her about how Adrian is my brother but we have different dads.

I tell her a bit about my mum and how pure evil she is.

Shevon rolls her eyes at me. 'She can't be *that* bad. At least you have food in your belly, that's more than some people.' Oh right, Shevon doesn't know about the cornflake sandwiches. I tell her about my dreams of being a rapper one day so I can prove all the horses wrong.

'Horses?' she asks.

'Yeah, the neigh sayers.'

'It's *nay*sayers, spelt N-A-Y,' she says. Whatever. She knows what I mean. I'll be the illest rapper and everyone in the naybourhood will love me and fist-bump me in the street.

Then I tell her about Shanks and how he's my OG but he's not very well right now and I ain't seen him in a minute, which is peak because it's summer and we were gonna do Raptology for the first time.

Shevon just listens to me ranting, she actually looks kinda worried.

'Well, if we're going to be lip-balm buddies –' she holds up the pineapple-passion – 'I can be your part-time bestie until your friend recovers.' I feel like my heart just went

Super Saiyan God level Ultra Instinct. We keep talking all the way back to Shevon's house. As we get closer to her yard, I try to walk slower, but we reach her gate anyway. I don't know if I should hug her or spud her hand, but it's OK because she's already on her doorstep with her keys.

'I had fun,' she says. She's busy tomorrow, but I can knock for her again on Wednesday.

'Yeah, that's cool, I think Wednesday works for me. I'll check my diary.' I have to buy one first. Before she goes inside, I have to get something off my chest, something that I've been wanting to say since Costa. 'Erm, Shevon?'

'Yes?'

'About before, I'm guessing you chose curtains for arms, right? Because you love your mum and that.' She giggles and shakes her head as she closes the door.

Homeless, Like a Slug
Next to a Snail

'You seem in a good mood today.' Mr Rix noticed I been buzzing since I came in this morning. And why wouldn't I be? I've got a new friend who my old friend will get to meet, and the three of us will be able to chill off at some point. I don't even mind it when Mr Rix brings out his classical music at lunchtime, it makes me feel like one of those posh lords in a mansion with a butler and a Rolls-Royce and a light in the bathroom that works. Swear down, every time I need to go toilet at night, I have to turn on the light in the corridor and keep the door wide open. For a number two, I have to close the door and use my phone torch.

Mr Rix wants me to get my vocabulary bigger, so he teaches me new words like 'exhilarating' and 'preventative'. Or sometimes he just tells me stuff about life, like how to do a tie that's not clipped on. Today he's got a different vibe though, he's asking me if I still want to be a rapper. I don't know if this is a trick question, like when Adrian told me to pull his finger, and I got so anxious I just farted on the spot. I'm probably just being para though, Mr Rix wouldn't do that to me. I can be honest.

'Man's been dreaming of them dollar-dollar bills since day.' I'll have to remind myself to change the currency to pound coins.

Mr Rix shakes his head slowly. 'As you grow, you'll hopefully learn that true wealth isn't in what you receive, it's in what you're able to give. Sounds to me like you're more passionate about money than you are about rap music.'

'No offence, sir, but how you so anti?'

'Being Black doesn't mean I *have* to be into a certain type of music,' he sighs, 'but I actually love rap, especially as a form of expression and celebration of culture. Shaun, music is something to be celebrated, enjoyed. I'd like you to try something, I want you to forget for a minute about the poolside models and the money. If they weren't on the cards, would you still want to rap?'

I take a second to think about it. 'Yeah, I would.' Going swimming would be more boring, but when I deep it, I'd still wanna be spitting bars. Rhymes just come to my head sometimes. I don't MC because I get paid, I do it for fun.

Mr Rix's eyes light up and he's nodding like someone just gave him a bowl of sticky-toffee pudding.

'Good.' He's smiling now. 'I hope you always remember that the art is infinitely more valuable than whatever lifestyle is attached.' Then he tells me about the history of rap. He thinks that if I really do want to be a rapper, then it's important to know the origins of the genre. Apparently it started with Jamaican immigrants going over to New York in the 1970s. He said that they would talk over tracks when they were introducing new songs, and loop beats over each other to create the track. I didn't know he could teach me so much about rap music. The only things I knew about rap history was that Busta Rhymes wasn't his real name, and 'hip-hop' is not short for 'hip-hoperation'. Bruh, this guy got me so invested I kinda wanna know more, like, what makes hip-hop bang so hard?

'The best rappers are storytellers as well as poets. I'm going to assign you some summer homework –' he grins – 'and I hope it has the same effect on you as it did on me. *Enter the Wu-Tang*, *The Chronic* by Dr. Dre and *Illmatic* by Nas – I want you to listen to these albums and pay attention to the themes and narratives. These guys paved the way for albums like *College Dropout* and future contemporary rappers like Kendrick and J. Cole.' Yo, Mr Rix is blowing my mind, he listens to Kendrick? 'The best rap isn't about self-hype and gun-toting, it's about telling a story. Remember that when you're onstage, will you?'

'Sir, how do you know so much about rap?'

'What do you think motivated me to become an English teacher in the first place? It wasn't just the holidays.' Swear down, I always thought he didn't want me to be a rapper, now he's telling me all of this? 'Shaun, I want you to decide your own fate, and not slavishly be what society tells you to be.'

I'm writing all the albums into the notes in my phone.

Before I go, Mr Rix tells me to try listening to new genres of music too, as they might influence my flow and introduce me to new beats. That's kinda long, there's so many whack tunes out there, even the birds in the park all have their own song, and I'm sure their lyrics are trash when you translate them into human. Crows would be the worst though, they'd get voted off every talent show, and probably cry in bed with that ugly sound they make. I guess Mr Rix is right though, he usually is, I should open my mind and my heart to new music and crows.

New music. Thought I knew music . . .

Classical? Wouldn't choose it.

I guess I'm switched on to light music,

I love chicken but I'm wrapped in rap music,

I'm lovin' the dollars but real scholars don't daydream to lose it, time to shift,

Mixin' it up coz I wanna pick bars apart from those tunes I hear in the lift.

* * *

School was actually live today, I'm strutting all the way down the street like I just got a fresh trim. When I get home, I head for the kitchen. Mum bought hot wings again, but they're kinda cold now. I put the food on a plate and sneak towards my room to watch TikTok compilations on YouTube. Mum says I'm not allowed food in my room, ever since she walked in and found me eating honey straight out the jar with my fingers because I wanted to see what it's like to eat like a bear.

I'm tiptoeing past her room and the door is a bit open. I can hear her saying something but it's not loud like when she's on the phone. I peer slowly around the door and see her sitting there, surrounded by letters that are all stamped red with 'Final Notice' written on them. My days, she's crying. She's muttering under her breath and she's crying. This is actually a madness. It's like one of those deeply mystical things that no one ever sees, like the back of a painting or a horse giving birth. I always thought I might enjoy seeing Mum cry because of all the times she's ruined my life, but this makes me feel crap.

I notice Adrian standing in his doorway. He puts his finger to his lips, telling me to be quiet, and beckons me over. It's got me kinda shook, still.

'What's going on?' I whisper.

'Fam, you haven't clocked? We're getting evicted.' One

look at his face and I know he ain't messing with me. My mouth drops open. 'Swear on my life, how have you not noticed that Mum's been in bare debt since she stopped working at the doctors' and started that cleaning job?'

'Evicted? Does that mean we're gonna be homeless?' My head is spinning.

'Maybe,' Adrian replies quietly.

OMG this is a nightmare. I picture my mum begging in the street with me and Adrian next to her, sleeping in a box. Oh God, what about Shanks? He's gonna come back and I won't even be here. I don't wanna leave the ends, my entire life is here. I can tell Adrian is thinking the same thing because for once he's not mocking me.

I'm not leaving. I swear on my life, I'm not going anywhere. I can't. Bruv, sometimes I get shook when we have to leave Zone 2 to go to them random places like Crystal Maze Palace. It's even worse when you leave Zone 6; you know you're far when they don't have Oyster card machines. We went to visit my uncle in Brighton once, and it was so far away that I had time to grow leg hair on my chest. I don't wanna move to Brighton and get initiated into a gang of fishermen, sea prison ain't the one. Fam, everywhere outside London looks the same; it's always just a high street with H&M and some houses either side. I make a promise to myself and a promise to Shanks. I'm not leaving.

So Much Beef the Steaks Are High

It's finally Wednesday, which means I get to see Shevon again. She takes ages to answer the door, and when she does it's on one of those chains that only lets you open it by a quarter of a fraction. I can only see half her face, and it looks like her hair and parts of her clothes are wet, like she's just been in a water fight. Behind her, I can see the house inside is dark like the Batcave, all the curtains are still closed.

'I'm really sorry, I can't come out right now. I want to, but I can't.' She's breathing heavily.

'Are you OK? Do you need help with something?' I ask. I can help. My mum says I have the problem-solving skills of a one-legged donkey, which is pretty useful because it means I could drag myself to safety. And I guess I could use my one hoof to stamp out a cigarette and prevent forest fires.

'I'm fine but I really have to go,' Shevon says. 'I'll be free for a bit on Saturday if you're around. I was thinking we could grab lunch. Let's say two-ish? There's an Italian restaurant we can go to in Camberwell that does the best carbonara.' She's talking so fast I can barely keep up. There's a loud thud like the sound of a sack of potatoes falling onto the floor. 'Gotta go.' Shevon slams the door in my face.

I slowly walk home, trying to make sense of what just happened. She seemed fine, she wasn't upset. But she was wet and out of breath. And then there's that thud that made her run back inside. The only logical explanation is this: a pigeon flew in through the window and Shevon tried to chase it out with a bottle of water. Two litres. Evian. When Shevon answered the door, the pigeon must have knocked over a sack of potatoes. I guess the real mystery is why they would buy bottled water instead of drinking from the kitchen sink or the bathroom taps like a normal person.

My stomach feels like it has an empty hole in it. I was kinda hoping to chat to Shevon about how I don't wanna move to Brighton and join a sea gang of pirates. I don't know the difference between port and starboard and Star Wars. She seems responsible, like someone who wears glasses, or washes Tupperware. Seeing her did brighten up my day, but it's cool, I'll chat to her on Saturday. We got time.

On my way home I turn left on Nigel Road and spot

something. Right by the playground, there's one of those big pushchairs, just left there. Being an MC is about seizing every opportunity, and I think I've just found one. I can spit a freestyle and show it to Shevon next time I see her. The hood on this push chair would make the perfect background for a quick sesh. Girls love rappers because of the poetry and lyrics, why else would they be in all the videos? There's no music or beat so Imma have to go acapocko. I wait for this guy to go past because I don't want him copyrighting my bars, and I strap myself in, pull out my phone and I start my greatest ever freestyle.

'Man is next though, let's go.

I might put 24 carrots on my bling like a rabbit, clear like a skylight,

My carrot gold get munched to highlight my dominant night-vision eyesight,

Shine bright like a rock, yeah I'm living a high life,

Diamond gal shine and she really be my type.

Bring it back like a repeat, we be in a teepee,

And she be bossing freely, sitting in sunlight.'

OK, that was one of the hottest bars that's ever been dropped. Off the dome, I just came up with that. Exotic bars like a Bounty.

Cool, let me bounce, I need to go home and write an exception speech for when I win an MTV award at the MOBO Awards. I go to unclip myself from the pushchair, but the thing is stuck. It's too tight and my finger won't press down hard enough to release it. I try again and again, pushing down on the clip as hard as I can, but it won't unstrap. Panic creeps in. I start to struggle but it doesn't change nothing. Across the road, a couple of girls have stopped walking and are looking over. Oh God no. I start getting frantic and try to wriggle myself free. It's still not working so I try to reach into my pocket. If I can stretch down enough, then maybe I can use my keys to saw the straps off. One of the girls is filming me now and they're both laughing. Some next man is walking towards me, but when he makes eye contact, he crosses the road. Damn. I finally touch my keys, but I fumble them and they drop to the ground. They sound like they landed under the pushchair, but I can't reach that far down. I try rocking backwards and forwards to get the chair to move so I can see the keys. Bruv, I'm sweating as more people join the girls across the road, I have to get outta here quick.

I think the only way out is to maybe shimmy up and out the straps because man's never gonna unclip this. It kinda works but my jeans are too thick. Out of instinct, I kick off my shoes and start wriggling myself up, out of my jeans and out of the pushchair. This was the wrong day to wear Y-fronts, I told my mum to stop buying me them. I wear boxers now. My trousers are around my ankles and people are openly laughing. I finally get to the point where my knee has popped out, if I can just get the other one free then I can stand up and climb out. I hear someone screaming over all the laughing.

'What the hell do you think you're doing in my son's pram?' Oh please God, no. A woman comes running out the playground carrying her kid. With her other hand, she starts beating me with her rucksack. As I get whacked, all the nappies and baby wipes and baby toys come spilling out. This makes her even angrier, and with every blow she's saying, 'Get. Out. Of. My. Baby's. Pram.'

I finally struggle free and take off down the road. Some people are cheering. I look back and see the woman gathering the stuff that fell out of her bag. I didn't have time to pick up my trousers or shoes, Mum's going to kill me. I sprint home without taking another look back.

Finally home, I get out the lift and run along the balcony. Adrian opens the door and sees me standing there in my pants and T-shirt.

'I'm not even gonna ask,' he says, and goes back inside.

I get a glass of water and slump into a chair. My legs are super tired, I can't remember the last time I got to just sit down somewhere. But then all of a sudden someone's knocking at the front door. I cba to get up and answer it. It's cool though, Mum's on her way. Before I can finish my water, I hear raised voices coming from outside so I get up to go peek round the living-room door. Beef on ends is always juicy; this one time, my neighbour's weave got dashed in a trolley because she threw someone's clothes out the window. True story.

I can hear Mum's voice getting louder. The front door's wide open and some tall guy in glasses is standing there with a clipboard under his arm. My stomach drops when I clock the council logo on his jacket, this visit must be formal. My guy looks like the type of wasteman who wears tight shorts and a fancy helmet when he cycles to work on a hot day. My mum is guarding the doorway, trying to block his view of inside. She's standing up straighter than usual, her arms are folded and she's using that weird polite but angry tone she sometimes has in the bank or at the post office.

'The letter said we still have a month to raise the money,' she's saying with her hands on her hips. That's when you know she means business.

'Yeah, good luck with that,' the glasses man says. He smiles as he notices me. Actually it's not even a smile; Mr Rix would call it a smirk, and it proper creeps me out, making my insides go cold and that. 'Is that your son?' He looks past her to stare me dead in the eye and says, 'Maybe you could talk some sense into your mum. It would be a shame to see you and all your belongings strewn out into the street.' My mum takes two steps forward, her hands clenched into fists.

'Don't you ever talk to my child. Don't even look at him, or I swear I'll slap your face into another reality.' The guy isn't even shook, he just starts strolling away without looking back.

'I'll see you soon, Ms Thompson, I'll see you very soon.' Mum hurries me away and sends me to do my homework.

But in my room I can't even bring myself to go on the PlayStation. I've got this pinching feeling in my stomach and chest. I didn't wanna believe Adrian about the eviction, but things are getting real out here.

I think about the man in glasses, how is he gonna talk to us like that? Fam, I need a quick way to make some bread. Whatever he wants, we need to pay it, otherwise he'll come back with an army of clipboards. And why was my mum having it from him? She only switched when he started sending for me. She was ready to throw hands because of me, it was proper exhilarating. But I'm also annoyed, because after all that beef, all that smirking from the guy in glasses, the council tryna kick us out like racism in football, after everything, I didn't get to properly record that freestyle for Shevon. Out of instinct, I reach for my phone to tell Shanks what just happened. I scroll down to his name before I remember he can't answer. I guess I'll just have to wait until Saturday and tell Shevon.

Veni Vidi Versaci

'Mum, can I have twenty pounds, please?'

'Ten pounds? What do you need five pounds for?' My mum is so annoying, she always does this. I do feel guilty asking Mum for P, like, we so broke that if I had a colouring book, I couldn't afford any mistakes. But I can't go out with Shevon if I don't have money to eat, and that would make me poor on the inside too.

'It's OK if you can't. I just wanted to go to an Italian restaurant in Camberwell.'

'Oh, now I know you lost your mind!' She laughs. 'What you doing sitting in an Italian restaurant for? You think you're Prince Harry?'

'No, I just wanted to go with a friend.'

'Oh.' Mum stops laughing and raises her eyebrows. 'You

have another friend?' I don't know if she's mocking it or not.

'Yes, I have a friend and her name's Shevon and she lives close by. Please, Mum, I promise I'll grow up and get a job and pay you back some day.'

Mum sighs and tells me to bring her handbag. I jump up and quickly hug her before running round the house to look for it. In the end, Mum only has fifteen pounds in notes, so she sits at the table and counts the rest out in coins. I'll pay her back by being interested in everything she says (because people love it when you pay them back with interest).

Walking through ends, I keep thinking of that guy in the glasses and all the people he's kicked out of their houses. All them families getting that knock. I'm still in my feelings when I get to Camberwell to meet Shevon.

The place is called Vertichellys. It doesn't even sound like a restaurant, it sounds like a Renaissance painter from the 1990s, it's kinda wavey. Inside, there's paintings on the walls and the chairs are actually made of wood. The people working here wear button-up shirts so you know they mean business, and the napkins are already folded on the table like tiny bedsheets. The waiter comes and pours some water without me asking; apparently it's free. I could get used to this, still. Shevon already knows what she's ordering – she barely even looked at the menu. She tells me she used to come here a lot with her mum.

'How do you know what anything is? There's no pictures.' I look around the room.

'The food is described in the menu,' she tells me.

I open the menu and I'm looking at it, but I can't read Italian.

'The menu's in English,' Shevon insists.

Don't watch that, there's some next words in here that don't match up with my lexicon. Even worse is the cost of everything. I'm looking at these prices and sweating like a fish (I know fish are sweaty, because whenever you see them out the water they're always wet). I hate being some broke guy, and I hate being evicted and I hate this stupid restaurant and their stupid prices.

'You OK?' Shevon can see me stressing. 'You seem a bit distracted.' I'm kinda a tiny bit excited that she can tell that something's wrong, I like that she's proper perspective like that. I start telling her about my mum losing her job and the guy in glasses, this council wasteman, who wants to kick us out. I don't wanna leave the ends, I know where everything is, and I need to be here for Shanks. I tell her that I think the only way to not get kicked out is to find extra cash to pay all that rent. But money isn't like potatoes, it don't grow on trees. Shevon says we can share a pizza because it's cheaper than getting one each, and we can share a starter too. I could see her eyeing up a carbonara pasta, and I don't want her to change what she's getting just for me, but secretly I'm gassed. Sharing a pizza with Shevon . . . I'm smiling like the cat from *Alice in Sunderland*.

When the waiter comes back, she orders us something called pro-ski-utto and a pizza I've never heard of before. Shevon leans back on her chair. I don't know how long the food will take, it could be anything from thirty seconds to over seven thousand seconds, which is probably almost a month in dog years, every year. I'm not sure what to do while we wait, but Shevon is trying to lighten the mood, being bare chatty, like one of those old ladies who works in Morrison's and is curious about the ingredients of my mum's tabbouleh. They're always like, 'Oh, couscous, I've never tried that before,' and I'm like, 'Yo, Mildred, chill. If I wanted small talk, I would talk to an ant. Because they're small.'

'So, what kind of food do you usually eat?' Shevon asks. 'I love Italian, and Thai as well. Me and my mum used to do one new restaurant every week.' She likes her food, boy. The only food I eat that's not Mum's cooking or school dinners is hot wings and chips, but I don't wanna tell her that.

'Yo, I love Italian food as well.' I guess that's accurate because I went to Pizza Hut for my birthday and it proper banged. 'My mum usually cooks real food on Sundays, but me and Adrian fend for ourselves during the week. Sometimes I have to get inventive with just a raw potato.'

It's not funny, but Shevon laughs anyway, and that makes me laugh a little bit too.

'What about your dad?' She takes a sip of water.

'I don't know him. He left before my mum got pregnant.' Shevon looks a bit confused. 'Do you have a dad?' I ask her.

'No, it's just me and my mum. He sends me money sometimes, which I get to spend on tasty food, but it's better that he's not around, to be honest. I'd rather have one happy parent than two unhappy ones.' She thinks for a second. 'Saying that, I'd rather have two happy parents than just the one. My life would be so much easier, you have no idea.' She looks away like she's daydreaming.

'My friend Shanks has a dad. Sometimes they go jogging together. I went with them once, but my legs didn't reach their full maturity. We had to keep stopping because I like to preserve my energy.'

The waiter interrupts us to bring olives and toothpicks. I think he's trying to finesse me.

'Yo, we didn't order this. I ain't paying for them.'

Shevon giggles nervously and tells me it's OK, but I don't want to pay for something I didn't order.

The waiter says they're complimentary. I don't know what that means, so he gives them to us for free. Cool. I feel a bit silly now.

Shevon tells me to try an olive, so I pick one up with my fingers; it feels like a plastic grape. I pop it in my mouth and chew it like a Starburst, and I almost break a tooth. There's a stone in it. 'Yo, what the heck is this?' I spit it out onto the plate.

Shevon's properly laughing now. 'You don't like it?'

'It tastes like deodorant.' That stuff is disgusting, no wonder the waiter gave it to us for free, that guy is a snake. Shevon's happily eating away though, still laughing at my reaction. Can't lie, this is actually kinda fun. I can feel my phone vibrating in my pocket, but it's probably just another prank call from the dentist.

My mood kinda dips when the food comes out though. The pro-ski-utto isn't even cooked, it's just raw meat. What am I, a lion? I know I smell like Lynx Africa, but I don't have the same dietary requirements as Simba.

Shevon happily eats the raw alien meat and olives while we argue over whether Nando's is better. We went there for Adrian's birthday. Like, Nando's has an actual spice scale. You can't measure how spicy Italian food is when there's no chilli scale for information. And for the record, I got extra hot. Lemon and herb is for wastemen who ride a push-scooter to work.

The pizza finally arrives and I almost wanna throw it across the room. This ting is thinner than the iPhone 14. There's no bread to it. And is that leaves? On a pizza? What is this, Kew Gardens? And an egg. Who puts an egg on a pizza? I ain't ever going to Italy if all they eat is raw ham and fertilized garden-centre pizza. Shevon's laughing at my reaction again. She can eat all the food and I'll just sit here huffing and puffing like a three billy goats gruff.

But even she can't eat all of it. 'Are you sure you don't want some?' she asks me when she's finished her half.

I tell her to get that devil food away from me. I just want to go KFC on the way home and wait for this hellish nightmare to end.

'Go on, try one bite, otherwise I'll just annoy you until you do.' She gives me one of those smiles where her lips are proper wide and red and touching. So I reach out to grab a slice of egg pizza and stuff it in my mouth to shut her up. The more I chew, the more I realise it's not actually that bad. I finish my slice and reach for another one out of instinct. She starts clapping and offers me some pro-ski-utto, but I choose life.

'So tell me, how are we going to raise the money to stop you from being homeless?' When she puts it like that, my stomach drops and I keep picturing the guy in glasses smirking at me.

'I don't know, fam. After that guy came to my yard the other day, I think we're running out of time.' We sit in silence while we both think.

'It needs to be something useful. Something like the weather app or online books,' she says.

'I don't think we need those,' I reply. 'If I want to know what the weather's like, I just look out the window.'

'Yes, but even if you do that, you don't know if it's going to rain in five hours' time.'

'Well, then I would just look out the window in five hours.' Why is making money so complicated? Rappers make it look so easy.

'OK, we're veering off-topic here. What's something that people need that they don't have?'

'Chewing gum. A pen. A good sense of smell. A hug.'

'Wow. That's a bit sad.'

'How is that sad? I'm not talking superhero levels, like smelling when a woman is pregnant.'

'Why on earth would a superhero need that particular power?' We go on talking about apps and money-making schemes and Shevon asks me if I want a coffee. I tell her I don't like coffee because I ain't a mum on the school run or a secretary working in fashion, and she looks disappointed. She says it's part of Italian culture to have one after the meal. Maybe I'm being too negative, I don't want Shevon to be disappointed, so when the waiter walks past, I call him over.

'Excuse me, kind bruv, do you have any Nescafé?' He looks like I just slapped him in the face with a pineapple pizza. 'Or do you do any fancy coffee?'

'I'm sorry, sir, our coffee machine is out of service today, we are unable to serve hot drinks right now.'

'Calm, I'll just have an iced coffee instead then.' Why is he frowning at me?

'Sir, there is no longer coffee on the menu.'

'Aite, fair. Can I have orange juice?'

'Yes. Pressed?'

'Nah, it's cool, take your time.'

He walks away, shaking his head, but it's just fresh Roman bantz. That guy's cool, I wish there was a way of showing waiters gratitude if you like their service.

After we finish our drinks, Shevon says we should pay the bill, but I tell her that we don't have enough to bribe the police. Turns out paying the bill has another meaning where I'm from. She wants to get the drinks because it was her idea, and I don't fight her on that because I'm a gentleman. As we leave the restaurant, Shevon's distracted by something across the road.

'That girl is staring at you,' she tells me. Well, I have been upping my workout. This morning Adrian caught me doing 2,000 press ups. Well, he called them 'unimpressups', but it still counts. I look over the road, and see a group of girls I recognise at the bus stop. Tanisha's friends are acting rowdy as always, but Tanisha is sitting a little bit away from them, looking over at us. The thing is, I ain't even excited to see her. Shevon asks if I know her.

'She's a girl in my class.' Shevon raises her eyebrow like she knows that there's more to the story. I tell her that me and Tanisha went cinema to eat yogurt, and then she finished me when Shanks did a madness online, and now we're kinda OK, I think.

'Well, do you want to go and say hello?' Shevon is wearing a yellow top and the sunshine just enhances her whole face like a day at the beach. I take one more look at Tanisha. She's bare peng, still, but the dragonflies in my stomach are hella quiet.

'You know what, I'm good.' We start walking away and I can see Shevon smiling to herself a little.

When we get back to her yard, we agree to meet up tomorrow to spend more time trying to come up with ideas to stop my family losing our house. I've got my hands in my pocket, I still don't really know how to say goodbye. Like, a handshake is too formal, I'm not King Charles talking to Meghan. But I can't really hug her, even though my mind is telling me to. And I definitely can't just wave, we ain't an old couple on a canal when boats go past.

We both hesitate outside her gate, it looks like we're about to hug but my arms won't comply. In the end, we both say, 'Goodbye,' and walk away with our hands by our sides.

Me and Shevon be side by side,
Her smile finds me and there's nowhere to hide,
Eat like a lion got mouthful of pride,
Man like pro-ski-utto, what you gonna do tho,
Take my heart on a ride.

Fine dining out here, ain't no barbecue rib,
Not all tasty olives but we live and let live,
Cornflake sandwich when you go back to the crib,
And I don't like her like that. But what if I did?
Don't watch. Bars, that's all I'm saying.

It's only when I start making my way home that I check my phone and see I got a call from an unknown number, it looks like they left me a voicemail. Skeen, no one leaves voicemails any more, this ain't the 1960s. I call it and my heart jumps up into my throat. It's Shanks, he left me a message. My chest is beating super fast while I hold the phone tight against my ear so I can hear every word. His voice is bare feebly as he says, 'Yo, Growls, sorry I must have missed you. I'll try again in a few days.' That's it, that's all he has to say. I play it over and over again to see if I missed anything, but I just keep hearing the same thing. The beating in my chest turns scratchy, I can feel condensation rolling from my eyes. That balloon in my chest that pushes the tears out is back. Why didn't I pick up? I was too busy laughing with Shevon, that's why, and Shanks has got no one to laugh with. I try not to imagine him on the other end of the phone waiting for me to answer. He's sad and lonely and sick, while I'm outside having fun in the world like a bouncy castle at a barbecue.

The next day I wake up extra early. I get a pen and paper from the drawer that's got all the batteries and old earbuds and that. I'm writing a letter telling Shevon that I'm sorry, but I'm too sick to leave the house today, so Imma have to link her another time. The sun is shining in my face while I walk round to hers and gently put it through the letter box so it doesn't make a noise. Damn, this would have been the perfect day to see her. But Shanks is still sick and I definitely don't wanna miss another call. If he can't have a new best friend, then I don't want one either.

Karen Dropping Knowledge Like Loose Change on a Bus

I'm in French class. I'm pretty sure that by the time I leave school in a few years I'll be able to do a proper good French accent. I'm also getting my French vocabulary bigger too, I already know words like 'cliché' and 'rendezvous'. There's a knock on the classroom door and Karen pops her head in, but I'm less nervous about our sessions by now. With all the stuff that's happening, I need to talk to someone, seeing as I can't talk to my mum about it, because she's always stressed about work and us being evicted, and she don't rate me like that anyway. And I definitely can't tell Adrian, he'll just call me 'Lady Jane' and say something like, 'Lady Jane cries in a puddle with her silly frilly dress-dress.' Sometimes when he bullies me, he takes it too serious and talks about how I got it easy because I'm young and I need to grow up. If growing up is so cool, then why do adults bend their knees to pick up heavy boxes like they're ducking a slow boomerang?

As soon as we get to her office, I put my bag by the door and take my seat opposite Karen. She asks me how I am and I just nod and say, 'I'm aite, fam, still.'

It's hard to concentrate when I got so much happening in my head. I know by now that the best way forward is to just say the thing that I'm thinking, and then things can get easier to understand. I take a deep breath in. Hold. Two. Three. And release. Karen does it with me, which is always funny because it makes me feel like one of us is giving birth. Puts me at ease though.

'So, I have a friend.' I hesitate.

Karen nods slowly and picks up her pen. She always writes new stuff in her notepad. 'You have a friend. It's not your friend Shanks?'

'No, it's not Shanks. But I was with her when I should have been talking to Shanks on the phone.' I tell Karen all about Shevon and how she's my new best friend and she makes me happy in a time where things aren't looking up. I tell Karen about the missed phone call, and how guilty I feel and the note I wrote to Shevon saying I couldn't come out. Honestly, chilling with Shevon is like being on a cool new planet, but Shanks is my brother, way more than Adrian. I just feel like I'm always doing the wrong thing.

'It's clear from what you're saying that your friends are important to you,' Karen says. 'Why do you think that is?'

'I guess, with Shanks, he's the only person I've ever met who never felt sorry for me or made me feel like I'm stupid. Shanks is the only person who never let me down. And he sees it too, I think, the way people look at me or talk to me. But he never copies them. He's never told me he's embarrassed to be my friend. He makes me think I could be liked.'

I never thought about it that way before, but it's true. And with Shevon, it's pretty much the same thing. She doesn't mock it, she seems to actually like me too. I don't get why she wants to chill with me, I'm not even cool or popular.

'Define popular,' Karen says. I tell her that it's when everybody likes you, gang-gang goals.

'And do you like yourself?' she asks. Whoa, that came out of nowhere. 'Take your time, you don't need to answer right away. Just think about it.'

Do I like myself? Yeah, I think I do. At least, I don't hate myself, and the opposite of hate is like.

'I for one agree, I think you are an exceptionally cool young man. As you grow up, you realise that popularity can be quite hollow, that although no one wants to be *dis*liked, you don't *need* to be liked either. The only opinions that matter are from those who know and love you the most. Everything else is fleeting.' She hitting me with some truths.

'Growls, you deserve this new friendship just as much as your friendship with Shanks. I get that you feel guilty about that call, I really do, but you are not betraying Shanks by developing a friendship with someone else. In fact, your avoidance of her means that all three of you are now missing out. And that doesn't really benefit anybody.'

Damn, this woman's good, sometimes it feels like she's reading my mind. If this was the 1980s, we would burn her steak for being a witch, and then she wouldn't have any steak #history #histronomical.

'What would you say to your friend if she was sat right here?'

I'm imagining Shevon sitting here right now, her red hair would look so cool next to this blue couch.

'I would tell her sorry, innit.' My voice is quiet, but I know the truth. It don't matter what happens with me and Shanks, my life is better with Shevon in it. The minute I see her, I'm running over to apologise.

'You remind me of my daughter,' Karen smiles. 'When she was your age, she had a big heart but she always kept people at arm's length.'

Skeen, keeping someone at arm's length makes it harder to do secret handshakes.

'What happened? I mean, to your daughter?'

'Oh, you know,' Karen responds happily, 'she grew up, just as you will, and now she's changing the world.'

'Like some sort of superhero?' I would be gassed if my kid was a superhero, I could be a parent sidekick; although I'm pretty sure that if I had powers, my mum would be the supervillain.

'Is my daughter a superhero? She is to me.' Karen laughs at my blank expression. 'After university she set up a social care charity. They do home visits for the vulnerable, helping them with the day-to-day chores that you and I might take for granted.'

'But how does that change the world?' I'm a little confused.

'By being there for people. Just being present is all it takes sometimes. Help one person smile, just one, and you can change everything. And in the same vein, you don't have to choose between your friends, you can be there for both of them.' Karen's tone is proper serious now. 'Growls, you are kind and reliable, and that makes you a hero in my eyes. You just need to show your friends that.'

Wow, Karen makes it sound so easy. But changing the world is a lot, that's more than seven countries full of people.

'Karen? You think I can be a superhero? Like in the same metaphor?'

Karen is positively beaming. 'Absolutely you can, Growls. You're full of energy, and you also have such a deep, caring soul in you. Like I said, sometimes the most heroic thing you can do is just to be there for people when they need you the most, that's all a relationship is. And that's true of friendships, romantic relationships, family relationships, everything. Just be present, open and honest. That's what a real hero looks like.'

'That's bare helpful, I think I can do that.'

There Is No 'I' In 'Apolog-Eyes'

I'm calling Shevon. Not on the phone, of course, because she doesn't have one, but I'm literally outside her house calling her name. As soon as school finished, I ran all the way here. My pens and my chewing gum fell out my pocket and I didn't even stop to pick them up. I'm at her door and I can't leave until I see her face. I put my rucksack on the doorstep and go to sit on it so that I don't ruin my school trousers, otherwise Mum will make me sew them up with a needle in a haystack. I can never find it.

Just as I sit down, the front door opens on that annoying chain link, so only half of Shevon's face is visible again. I jump straight back up.

'What do you want?' she says through the gap in the

door. Just seeing a part of her angry face makes my chest feel like a Drake song.

'Shevon, I'm sorry for the other day.'

'Yeah, you should be, that really sucked. I was looking forward to seeing you.' That makes me feel a million times better and a million times worse.

'I know, and I was looking forward to seeing you too. I'm always looking forward to seeing you. From the moment you close that door and I run home, I'm looking forward to seeing you.'

'Why do you run home? Why can't you just walk?' She almost smiles for a minute, but then she goes straight back to being vexed.

'Look, I had an apostrophe,' I tell her. She just looks at me like she don't know what I'm saying. 'It means, like, I had a realisation.'

'I think you mean an epiphany.'

'Nah, it's not Christmas. Shevon, I just want to be around you. I like chilling with you and I like being around you.' I'm staring at the floor but I can feel her eyes watching me. Sometimes I feel like she can read me like a book, which is funny because I can't even read a book like a book. Bruv, why is this so hard? I can't think, I can't find the words; this is like a game of Scrabble. 'OK, you remember I told you about my friend Shanks?' She nods. 'Well, in the back of my mind, I thought that being friends with you was kinda betraying him in some way. But I can be there for both of you. And I'm the luckiest person in the world because I have two best friends instead of one.' The door closes and I hear her run upstairs. Wow, I think I've blown it. I pick up my bag to turn and leave, but then I hear the chain fumbling and then the door swings wide open. Shevon just stands there holding the pineapple-passion lip balm that I gave her in Costa.

'What was all that drivel about being best friends?' She nudges me playfully and I can feel a super huge smile on my face. 'By the way, my name is spelt S-I-O-B-H-A-N, you've been spelling it wrong this entire time.'

Lol, that's ridiculous. There's no 'B' or 'H' in Shevon. Otherwise you'd say it like 'Shen-ha-bonovon'.

'Trust me on this one, I know how to spell my own name,' Siobhan says. Well, that makes one of us. I know how to spell 'Shaun' and I know how to spell 'Thompson', but my middle name is something like Bethany Ezeekeeyal Frenkel.

Ezeekeeyal, keeping it real.
Real name game but it's neeky, man like zeeky-E,
It's freaky like Friday for real, turned it round like a wheel,
Siobhan is back like an apple and I see the ap-peel,
On my knees begging but my name isn't Neil,
Now I'll fly like a fish, that's how Siobhan makes me feel.
Don't watch that. That was from the dome *and* the heart.

'You got any plans for the rest of the week? Maybe we can hang out after you finish school.'

'I'm not about tomorrow,' I tell her. 'My mum said I have to look after my two cousins while my Aunt Tina has a job interview.'

'Holy crap, an adult actually trusts you with their kids?'

'Adult? Clearly you've never met my Aunt Tina. She went out with my mum one time and got so drunk she started dancing on the table.'

'She sounds like fun.'

'They were in a massage parlour.'

'Oh.'

'Yeah, and there was another time they were doing the limbo.'

'The limbo? Come on, that sounds pretty harmless.'

'She limbo'd under some police tape and farted in a crime scene.'

'Oh,' she says again, then changes the subject. 'You got a picture of your cousins?' I pull out my phone and scroll through the pictures until I find one. Obviously I breeze past the selfies because Siobhan's not ready for those. They're for when I sign my first record label and I need a gorgeous album cover. 'They're adorable, how old are they?'

'Jordan is nine, and I don't know how old Rochelle is.'

'Oh, OK. Well, which one's older?'

'Neither, they're twins.'

'Then they're the same age, you joker.'

'Oh right, yeah. Geez, can you imagine what it's like to have twins? I could not handle being pregnant for, like, nineteen months.'

'What?' She shakes her head. 'No, you'd still only be pregnant for nine months. And by the way, two times nine is eighteen. That's silly even in your logic.' Someone calls through the open front door. Siobhan tells me to wait a sec and disappears inside. I think it's her mum and I can hear Siobhan saying that she's with a friend.

'Cool, is that your mum? I can come in and say hello,' I say when she comes back out.

Siobhan immediately puts her hand up to block the door. 'You can't, she's busy. And I have to go make dinner, but give me your hand, I want you to have this.' She pulls out a pen and starts writing a foreign number on my palm. 'It's not foreign, it's a landline. If you call this number, I'll probably pick up.'

'Skeen, what if you don't have reception?'

'It's a house phone, it doesn't need reception.' Wow, OK. A phone that doesn't need reception. Maybe Siobhan is in touch with modern technology after all.

The entire way home I don't put my hand in my pocket or do anything that might smudge the phone number. I got these summer tunes playing in my ear that make me think even more of Siobhan and the way she looks at me. My mouth smiles when I think of her, even though I'm not asking it to.

When I come inside, I can hear voices in the kitchen. It's only Mum and Sharon, who's our next-door neighbour except that she lives three doors down. So I guess she's our next door's next-door neighbour twice removed. I have a cousin who was twice removed, but that was for armed robbery.

The best thing about Sharon is the way she talks, it's all like, 'My 'usband, 'arry, wears 'is sun 'at when 'ees on 'oliday.' It gives me proper lols. Mum's always got her arms folded when they're talking, nodding along even though I know she don't understand a single word.

Any time anything happens on ends, Sharon knows about it. When Cyril from number 84 got nabbed with Younger Knuckles for crashing that shopping trolley, Sharon knew about it. And when Samuel who lives in Stansfield House got chased by the feds for shooting fireworks at people, Sharon was the one who was filming. And when Adrian was charged with Miss DeMeaner, Sharon was the one who called my mum. I like her, she's always been kinda safe to me and Adrian. She's like a character out of *EastEnders*, except a drumbeat and the theme tune don't start playing when she stops talking.

Right now she's talking about this guy in the glasses, the council guy who wants to kick us out. Apparently Sharon saw him knocking while I was at school. I guess Mum must've been sleeping; she does that during the day now, like a bat or a security guard. It makes me shudder when I think of him tryna come round again.

''is name's Gregory Flynn, and it ain't the first time 'ees done this.' This man's got two first names, that's how you know he's not from ends. He's happy kicking us out of them though. Sharon says the council are useless as a chocolate teapot, and tells Mum that we should ask Citizen's Advice. Allow it, we went there before, when Adrian got in trouble, it's just a waiting room with no air conditioning. I'm not a fan. 'You remember Sally who used to live at the end of the landing, number 84? When 'er youngest was born, she 'ad to quit 'er job, the kid was terribly ill, she was. Well, that guy, Gregory Flynn, was at the front door before Sally's P45 was even in the mail.' She shakes her head and Mum looks worried, biting her nails. 'Nasty piece of work,' Sharon continues. 'Preys on the most vulnerable, elderly couples and families with young kids, people like that. You'd best be careful with 'im.' Geez, if there's one thing Sharon hates, it's the council. And the letter 'H', but I think she hates the council more.

I get to my room, flop down on my bed and carefully add the landline number written on my hand into my mobile and save it as 'Siobhan'. I stare at the number a little bit before I lock the phone and turn on the PlayStation. Can't lie, hearing Sharon talk about this Gregory Flynn guy has got me panicking. If he can evict a woman and a new baby, he'll make light work of my family.

16

I'm Not Egyptian But I Love My Mummy

Wednesdays are the worst. I have double maths in the morning, then geography with Mrs Oh Riley, and back-to-back IT lessons in the afternoon. I know you're thinking IT isn't that bad, but it is when all the cool websites are blocked. We can't go on YouTube, Insta or any streaming sites. It's like being back in the middle ages, when all they had was news sites and emails. Apparently in the Victorian times, when Queen Elizabeth was still about, they didn't even have Wi-Fi. Instead they had bikes with one huge wheel and one tiny one, so you could only chain it up to a wall that was, like, twenty feet high. If you take away Wi-Fi, you're taking away my human rights, which is the only thing that sets us apart from animals and ghosts. Yeah, that's a no from me #thankyounext.

Ever since I started chilling with Siobhan, the time's been going bare quick. There's only a week left at school before the summer and I get to throw my timetable away. Then I think about Raptology and my stomach drops because it reminds me of Shanks. His chair is still empty like a bottle of Coke Zero because there's none left. I missed his call four days ago and I ain't heard nothing since.

When I pick up my cousins from school, they're on a proper hype. Jordan has a pound on him, so I let him buy sweets to help calm them down. Bruv, primary-school kids are the worst. Why are their hands all sticky? Once we're indoors, they go running upstairs to get out their uniforms, and I sit in front of the TV to catch up on some YouTube. It's not too long before my Aunt Tina comes home. She asks me if I want to stay for dinner, but these kids are too rowdy. I say that I'd rather eat cornflakes with a pair of chopsticks out my own bellybutton. She laughs and says that actually sounds kinda sophisticated. I might try it.

They only live on Yellowbrick estate, so it's not too far for me to walk home. Aunt Tina offered to have us stay with her if we do get evicted, but the place just isn't big enough. Mum doesn't wanna share a sofa bed with me and Adrian. I get it, Adrian's a sleepwalker, he once slept walked all the way to a house party at 3 a.m. and then bopped all the way home.

When I get in, I put my bag down by the door as usual,

but it's odd. Everything is quiet. Mum's usually watching TV at this time. It's her ritual before she leaves for work. I sneak down the corridor and peek into her room. The curtains are drawn and I see her body breathing.

'Mum? Are you OK?'

'Not now, child. Let me lie down a while. Go help yourself to some snacks from the cupboard,' she says. The other day she mentioned she was taking longer shifts, and I know she's been extra tired since then. But her voice sounds more than just tired. Maybe I should see if everything's OK. After all, I mean, she has raised me by herself, worked night shifts every day to feed me and Adrian, turned up to almost every parents' evening, washed us and fed us, day in, day out for all these years. But on the other hand, we *do* have some decent snacks in the cupboard . . .

As I carry the crisps and chocolates back to my room, I go past my mum's door again. You know what, this doesn't feel right, my mum would never give me free rein with the blessed snack shelf. I look at her room and I look at the snacks. Damn. I go put them back on the shelf and say a little prayer for their safety from Adrian.

I decide to make Mum a camomile tea. I haven't made it before, but I know how she takes her tea – milk, one sugar – so hopefully that'll make her feel better.

She doesn't answer when I knock so I just walk in. She's bare shocked when she opens her eyes and sees me standing there with the mug of inky egg water. I tell her it's camomile when really it's only cam-a-few-metres.

'What's this for?' She's proper surprised. I tell her I brought it in because she might be sick. 'I'm not sick,' she sighs. 'I told you, you can go get a snack from the cupboard.'

I hesitate. 'I don't want anything from the cupboard.' That's definitely a lie.

'Well, what do you want?' My mum is eyeing me up suspiciously. Why she always paranoid for?

I don't know what to say, I'm making this up as I go along. I just want her to get out of bed. Losing her receptionist job and then all this annoying house stuff has pushed her to the edge. I miss the days when we were all less stressed out. When I was little, Mum used to laugh more. On the weekends she would take us to the park or to random places like museums or IKEA. We'd play all day, and then at night she'd make our favourite beef stew as a treat. That was when she was happiest. I miss that Mum..

'I want to make Nanna's beef stew.'

'Boy, you don't know how to make Nanna's stew.' She looks into the mug and immediately puts it on the bedside table without taking a sip.

'Well, maybe you can show me?'

Mum sits upright in her bed. Finally, some proper movement.

'You want *me* to show you how to make Nanna's beef

stew? You know that was your great-grandma's recipe.' She toys with the idea in her mind. 'Well, Adrian's hardly gonna learn, that boy tried to cook a frozen pizza with the packaging still on.' She sighs and starts getting out of bed. 'Right, come on, let's do this before I change my mind.'

I didn't know cooking could be so fun. Mum needed a few more ingredients, so I ran to Mr Ravi's shop while she started prepping. I was bouncing on the spot while he counted all the coins. When I got home, I burst through the door with my shopping bag. Mum was already cutting up beef and listening to old school R'n'B. She got me chopping garlic, celery, and these purple onions called shallots. I joke to mum that I read a book in English class called Shallots Web. That joke was fire. Mum clears her throat and carries on chopping. Snake. The tomato paste proper disintegrates like a vampire walking into a church on some supernatural wave.

She cooks the beef until it's brown on all sides, and then places it into the other pot with all the bay leaves and peppercorns and tomato paste. The whole place smells amazing, it smells like home, just like when Nanna used to cook for us. She looks at me proudly as we cover it and turn the heat up. I'm super happy because we did it together, but then it gets really sad when I think about why it's not like this all the time.

'You OK, son?' She flaps the oven mitts over her shoulder. Boss move.

'Yeah, I guess.'

She doesn't believe me. 'Boy, I didn't raise no liar.'

I guess she's right, technically she raised two.

'It's fine,' I tell her. She raises her eyebrow. 'Seriously, Mum, I've got a counsellor now, we don't need to talk about it.'

Mum bites her tongue as if she's about to shout, but then she takes a deep breath. 'I'm glad you're opening up to your counsellor, but I'm your mother. You can talk to me.'

'It doesn't feel like that sometimes.' I'm looking at the ground. 'I never see you any more, which I get because of work and that, but when I do, you're always hella stressed. I never wanna disturb you, and whenever I'm in the house I feel like I haven't got anyone to chat to.' The steam from the stew creates moisture on my eyes and the water rolls down my cheeks.

Mum takes two large steps towards me, grabs me into a big hug and pulls me close. 'Don't you ever feel like you can't talk to me.' She shakes her head. 'I'm sorry I haven't been around much. It's all this stress from the council.' She cuts off, taking a deep breath. 'And with all that was going on with your friend, I should have asked how you were doing.' She sounds so tired. But I guess she's only tired because she works so hard. She doesn't do it for bants, she's just trying to make sure me and Adrian don't starve. Even though she's always stressed, this is her way of being there for us. And that makes her a superhero too. 'Shaun, I should have asked how you were doing, and I'm sorry.' She cups my face with both hands, just like she used to. I close my eyes because it reminds me of a time when we used to be happy, when we had each other's backs, when it felt like we were a family. 'I've not given you any time, not to you or your brother, and that's not fair of me.'

I hug Mum tight. Her perfume is flowery, and it reminds me of once when I fell asleep on her lap during a car journey from the airport. She spent that entire journey stroking my hair and playing on her phone. More tears come down my eyes because that car journey feels like so long ago.

'Do you like me, Mum?' My voice is bare whispery.

'Shaun –' she leans back so she can look me in the eye – 'I love you. If you need reminding of that, then I'll try to show it more. You'll always be my son. And as soon as we can, I'll take you to see your friend. Shanks, that is, not the girlfriend Adrian saw you with.'

Rix It for a Chocolate Biscuit

Today at school feels kinda strange. Mum gave me extra dinner money when I left the house, as if she's a millionaire like Tony Stark. I'm not complaining, it's just never happened before. I finally got a text message from Shanks too, telling me he's doing better and asking me how I am and that. He sent me a couple tunes he's been listening to, and one of them is pretty decent. He says he's well enough to talk later and I'm so excited that I spin on the spot and do the peace sign like an anime character. The dinner lady just looks at me all confused, her mouth hanging open, and slowly hands me my change.

Lunchtime with Mr Rix is calm as usual. Even though the kids aren't really mean any more, I think I got into the habit of chilling here during break. Mr Rix don't really complain, I guess I must've misunderestimated him. I tell him about my mum while we both munch down on our sandwiches. I tell him about how new and good it felt to do something with her, even if it is just cooking.

'I'm glad you had a good night,' Mr Rix says in between bites of food. 'You mentioned you two haven't always gotten along, or have I misheard?'

'Lol, sir, that's like saying cats and dogs haven't always gotten along. And if I was a cat, then my mum would be a house fire that I came crawling out of, all ashy and burned, and then I cough some little cloud of black smoke. It's been like that a lot lately. Except for last night and this morning she wasn't.'

Yesterday felt like things can change. Adrian's always telling me that he's the man of the house and I have it easy, but maybe I need to support Mum a little bit. After what Karen said, maybe I can be her hero too. Mr Rix just nods in silence. 'It's just, I know she's going through it right now, and she's been stressed, and me and Adrian don't make things easy. But this might be the beginning of a fresh start, and I don't want to mess that up.'

Mr Rix sighs and stands up. He goes to stand by the window and asks me to join him. 'Shaun. Look over there. You see that tree?'

Of course I see it. It's a massive tree.

'Yeah, sir. It's pretty hench, still.'

'It's quite glorious, isn't it?' I don't know where he's going with this.

'Yeah, I guess.'

'Now look closer. You notice how all the leaves are different colours? Where the sun hits it, there are a million different greens all happening at once.'

'Yeah, I can see that.'

'And the bark, do you think it's smooth and sleek?'

Bruh, it's a tree. But I think about when I was young and scratched my arm running past a tree in Dulwich Park. 'Bark isn't smooth, it's bare rough, and it hurts.'

'Right, but regardless of all the different coloured leaves and the rough bark, that is still a very wonderful tree, is it not?' I guess he's right. The branches are swaying a little bit, but the more I look, the more I see how amazing it is. 'Shaun, your mum might have been imperfect in the past. As have you, as have I. But despite her rough bark and her mismatched leaves, she is *your* mother. Listen, my point is, people are like trees. We each have our role, we're each beautiful and full of colour. But we're also rough and each of us is different. Some things are perfect *because* of their imperfections, not despite them.' I think of Siobhan and the way she crinkles her nose when she concentrates. And then I think about my mum. She's also a tree because she's not perfect, but she is my mum, and she's beautiful.

'So, sir, does that mean that my brother would be one

of those dead Christmas trees with, like, three branches for the decorations?' I expect him to be a little angry, but Mr Rix just laughs.

'Your notion of beauty changes as you get older. I think if people were always exactly as you'd want them to be, the world would be a boring and predictable place.'

He's right about the tree, and I can't stop staring at it, it looks like it's got its arms wide open like someone waiting for a hug.

'*King of Finland coz I'm Finn King out loud.*

Pirate gang got me inland out, two's a couple,

Trees a crowd, me, mum and Adrian and we won't go without

Breaking out of this cycle coz the chains won't hold out.'

Yo, I forgot Mr Rix was there. His eyes are wide and he's grinning like he's impressed. I can't look him in the eye.

'Keep that energy up,' he says. 'I mean it, I think you have a real talent, and I'll help nurture it in any way that I can.' Can't lie, part of me is low key excited when he says that.

The phone is ringing and my heart is pounding in my chest. I don't know what I'm going to say.

'Hello?' Shanks sounds like he's just woken up, but it's him, it's my best friend. I close my eyes and imagine we're standing next to each other, picturing his little, pretty face with that cheeky boy island smile.

130

'Yo, fam, it's me.'

We immediately start talking at the same time at a million miles per hour, saying, 'Oh my days, how you doing, bro?' and, 'I miss you, bro, how are you?' and we just keep doing this over and over again until we both pause for breath.

Then Shanks says, 'Growls, I miss you so much, man. For real, I miss chilling, bro, things are so mad, but I can't wait to get better and come check you.'

'Yo, where you at? Is everything OK? Bruv, I can hop on a bus and see you, I'll bring a Ribena or those barbecue wings you like. Are you still in the hospital? I ain't heard nothing, and, bro, I can't believe it's actually you right now.' Yo, I'm so gassed, Shanks is back.

'Nah, I was for, like, a while, but I'm home now. It's better if you don't visit me though. I proper want you to, but my mum don't think it's a good idea yet. I'm still not fully better.'

'Yo, it's cool, fam, you don't have to explain. I just can't wait to see you. Promise you'll come out and kick ball when you can?'

'I triple promise. Bruv, it's so wild to chat to you. How's the fam?' I tell him about how I cooked with my mum and he asks me to repeat myself because he thought he misheard. Then I tell him everything, about Karen and Siobhan, but I don't wanna worry him about the eviction stuff. I kinda wanna mention the Raptology competition we were supposed to do, it's coming up real soon, but I don't wanna put that on him either. There's no point anyway, he's locked up at home, and probably not well enough. The chances of us performing are slimmer than my Aunt Tina when she forgot to top up her gas card and accidentally did intermittent fasting. I don't mind though. Now that I've heard Shanks' voice, I'm double sure we're not going anywhere.

'Growls, this Siobhan, do you, like, fancy her?' Shanks is diving straight in there, boy, don't watch that. I wanna sing Siobhan's name and tell him that I can be myself around her. Like, I can eat a plate of buffalo wings to completion in front of her and not have to wipe my mouth in between. Instead, I ask him about when he was in hospital and if it's true that nurses are all hot and wear tiny dresses. He tells me his nurse was called Steven, and a lot of nurses wear dead crocs. And they don't wear tiny dresses like on Halloween, they wear scrubs that look like blue kitchen towels with a V-neck. We talk about football, and about my lunchtimes with Mr Rix, and my hardcore workout routine that I definitely do. When he tells me he's only got a few minutes before dinner, it almost sounds like he's in prison, but I got to go anyway. Mum cooked a Spanish pie from her recipe book that's got rice and prawns and stuff in it. I think it's called pie-ella, and you can't cook it with salmon because you could get salmon-ella. What kinda madness is that? Allow getting food poisoning from something that doesn't even look like a pie.

'It's not strange if you're in Spain.' Shanks laughs. 'They would probably think it's strange to eat as much fried chicken as we do. Anyway, I got to go, but bell me at this time again next week.'

'I will. And Shanks . . .' How do I say this without sounding like a wasteman? 'I miss you like a waterfall misses the summer moonlight.'

'I miss you too, fam. In a bit, bruv.'

'Yeah, in a bit, my G.'

Leonardo DiCaprio and the Sixteen Chapels

'Yo, Siobhan, what's the place we're going to?'

'It's the National Gallery in Trafalgar Square.'

'You know if the mandem see me there, my street cred is ruined,' I tell her.

Siobhan rolls her eyes. 'Let's assume your "mandem" are there. It would be a miracle if you had any to begin with, and an absolute coincidence that they'd be in the gallery at the same time that we're there.'

I flop back in my chair on the bus. Why she trying to logic my life on public transport? She wants to be an artist one day, and she comes to these moist galleries and museums for inspiration. I'm just here because it's free and I get to chill with Siobhan.

'Art isn't moist. Who do you think designs the album

covers for those rappers you listen to? Who designed the football kits of the players you like? And it's not just that – art is about identity and true expression in a time where those two things are so important. I honestly think there's an artist in all of us.'

'Bruh, you lost me at "art isn't moist".'

'Well, I think you're moist for saying that. Press the bell, we're almost here.' Siobhan gathers her stuff and stands up so we can finally get off. We cross the road onto Trafalgar Square. I never noticed how big it is. Maybe it just looks smaller on my TV because we only have a 32-inch screen. There's all these neeky tourists everywhere in brightly coloured coats and rucksacks that anyone in South East would get bullied for wearing. Seriously, if I was on a plane and needed a parachute and the only ones they had were in those rucksacks, you'd best believe Imma strap myself in, check the Ryanair sandwich menu and wait for Iron Man to save me.

I'm bare gassed when we pass the four statues of a lion pride #spiritanimal #holyhowlerini. I wonder which one of the lions is called Nelson. I really wanna climb on one, but Siobhan drags us to the building on the far side of the square and up a million stairs to the entrance. When we get to the top, my energy bar is wiped out. She doesn't even notice, she just carries on inside. I really wanna rest up and chill until closing time, but Siobhan was really excited about showing me a different art form, so I firm it like an unripe avocado and follow her in.

Yo, this place is huge, somehow it feels even bigger than being outside. I notice the security guard watching us closely as we're walking in. As if I would steal one of these paintings – even the small ones wouldn't fit under my hoodie.

The ceilings in here are so high it feels like a cathedral, like when Leonardo DiCaprio painted the sixteen chapels; I wonder if that's in here. Bruh, the paintings are nothing like how they look on TV either, it's like they've been enhanced to the size of a building and put in HD. Some of these must have taken more than three hours for the artist to paint.

'Three hours? Try years.'

'Siobhan, three years is more than three hours, isn't it not?' Hah, gottem.

The rooms we're walking in are bigger than my whole house. For real, at home, if we order a large pizza, we have to eat it outside. My house is so small, if LeBron James lay down in my bed his feet would be poking out the front door. Wow, LeBron James in my house. My house. That I might not live in much longer. I need to think about something else . . .

What's annoying is that next to every big painting there's a tiny piece of art that's just words on a bit of paper.

'Seriously? Those are the descriptions.'

'Why would I need a description when I can see the real thing right there?'

'It gives you important information, like names and dates.'

'Who cares about dates? Calendars are really just more of a suggestion anyway.'

'They're really not.'

'Oh yeah? Then why does the dentist let me reschedule any appointments that I miss?' Siobhan rolls her eyes, but I can see her smile. As she walks further ahead, I can't help but think that her smile is way better than any of the ones in these paintings.

I think Siobhan's legs are getting tired, so I sit down on one of the benches in the middle of the room while she wanders around. It's so funny to see her next to all the grown-ups, looking at the paintings with a tiny intelligent frown on her face that looks like she can smell a fart. She's so smart, I'm sure one day she'll grow up and be the first female Prime Minister. Maybe I could be her hench bodyguard and help her out of cars or hold her hand while we walk along a beach. She comes over to sit down and nudges me with her knee.

'See anything you like?'

'Yes,' I reply. Her eyes are so kind and lovely, and her eyebrows are on point like she probably got them threaded recently.

Siobhan blushes and looks away, like a sun-dried tomato

turning to face east. 'Paintings,' she says. 'Are there any paintings you like?' Oh. Right. That. 'I think of some of these paintings as a window into the past, or as a kind of spiritual beauty that only human creativity and talent and patience can make. Gosh, I hope I can do this one day. How does it make you feel?'

'Yeah, these paintings are cool and that, like better than I thought, but I'm never gonna be the next Galileo Figaro or the next Vincent Van Damn or the next El Salvador Darling. I can't even draw a bath.' It's true, the paper gets wet from the moisture in the bathroom, and Mum's always banging on the door, distracting me. Just thinking about my house gives me these needles in my chest. But Siobhan said that we're both artists, and if we're here for inspiration, then I should try and focus on that.

'Shaun?' Siobhan says my name and the needles start dying down. Well, she used my birth name but still, I'm sure even J-Lo gets called Jemima sometimes. 'Whenever I'm feeling overwhelmed, I find that artwork takes me out of the real world and shows me that anything is possible, the same way it does with your music. I'm just saying, if an artist has a talent, and I guess they work at it, then sooner or later things will get better.' Siobhan puts her hand on mine, in a comforting way, and in the moment I feel like I can do anything. She stands up, still holding my hand, and pulls me to my feet so we can continue the tour.

Because we walk at different speeds, we spend the rest of the time usually on opposite sides of the room or crossing each other on the way in and out. Sometimes I catch her watching me and she looks away, and sometimes I'm watching her and she notices, so I pretend to look at a painting.

Right now I'm looking at a painting of a horse. Bare detailed and that. But the horse is massive, this painting is three times bigger than me. It's like the horse is looking into my soul. I lean my head left and right and the horse is still looking at me. Some noble steed, boy. I can't stop staring at it. If the horse had a theme tune, it would be one of those classical music songs that Mr Rix is always playing. In my head, I think about how the horse is also kinda gangster, so I add drum and bass to the tune in some epic remix. I shout, 'Reeeeemix' like a DJ when the beat drops, and everyone in the gallery tells me to shush.

This painting though, it almost makes me feel strong, like somehow I can be the horse. This isn't about a horse, or a painter, it's about me. Siobhan said there's an artist in all of us. She wasn't just talking about painting. I turn to look for her, but she's already standing right next to me. I can relax.

'There's no reason we can't all produce something as beautiful as this. None,' Siobhan whispers, more to herself than to me.

And she's right. I think about my passion, what is my version of this? I'm Growls. Growls, who growls like a tiger before his rhymes. I am a lyricist; my words are like my paintbrush.

'You know, I used to think that rapping was about getting paid and popping bottles, gang-gang, but it's not like that. It's funny you brought me here, my English teacher is always tryna make me see true art in my lyrics. The passion is real out here.'

Siobhan agrees, she's nodding along. 'What was that competition you were telling me about, ages ago in Costa? The one where you battle onstage or something.'

'Raptology?'

Siobhan says she thinks it's a good idea for me to do it, maybe it'll take my mind off the eviction. And that studio time for the winners would be the perfect way to launch my first EP. The competition's only two weeks away though. I take out my phone and show Siobhan the official profile on IG.

'Um, Shaun?' Her eyes are wide and her mouth is hanging open as she scrolls. 'You do realise there's a cash prize?'

What?

My days, it's actually on their official page. She's pointing to their pinned post, where in big letters it says: 'First prize: £3,000 and 12 hours studio time.' Wow.

'Are you thinking what I'm thinking?' Siobhan says.

'Yeah. Do animals know when it's their birthday?' Wait, that's not it. I bet dolphins do though, and mermaids before they went extinct. Siobhan has her hands on her hips, waiting for me to catch up. 'Why don't aeroplanes have wings that flap?' Bruh, I have no idea. I mean, wait, pause, rewind, we were talking about Raptology, about a tonne of cash, gang-gang, ballah dropping bills on ma way to the club.

No.

Money to save the house.

I can use the money to save the house!

Siobhan is grinning and nodding, and I do a little victory dance where I cut shapes like a skanking machine. This could be my one shot, my opportunity to sneeze on everything I never wanted, to capture ships, or just let it rip. Siobhan's a heroic level boss. She wanted me to figure it out for myself.

But then my heart sinks. 'What about Shanks?'

'You guys are super tight, why don't you just ask him if you can do it without him?'

I'm scared, what if he says no?

Siobhan shrugs. 'Send him a message. Maybe you can even visit him?'

'I think he's doing better, like, I chatted to him on the phone. Still, he might need to ask his parents.'

'Well, you don't know if you don't ask.' She's right. And she's so extremely beautiful with her eyes and her eyebrows and long messy hair. I don't know how, but

Siobhan is so confident. And I don't mean 'confident' like a girl who shouts stuff from the roof of a limo on her birthday, I mean it in a good way. I dunno, things make so much sense when she says them. I know me and her are just friends, but I can tell you now that my friendship with Shanks doesn't make me feel the same way.

A Phone and a Wedding?
That's a Ring-Ring Situation

We get off the bus back in the ends, and I feel my entire body start to relax. I'm home. There's just something comforting about seeing the corner shop, seeing mandem ride their bikes freely, the graffiti, even the yardie man selling juice from his shopping trolley. Today was pretty decent though. That painting of the horse is still fresh in my mind and it makes my heart sing like a hummingbird.

I walk Siobhan back to her squeaky gate and she turns to me.

'There's something I've been meaning to ask you.'

Oh.

'Whatever it is, the answer's yes. Unless it's a maths question.'

'It's not a maths question, silly.' OK, cool, numbers are the worst. 'Listen, my uncle on my dad's side is getting married. I don't really wanna go but my mum thinks I should, and she said it would be a good idea, if I'm nervous, to invite you. It's next Saturday if you can make it.'

Wow. I've never been to a wedding before. I've been to two funerals, and my cousin's home birth when the Uber driver turned up at the house and was like, 'Nah, G.' Hopefully this will be different.

'So you'll come?' she asks.

'Yeah, that sounds good, I think I can make it,' I say in my deepest voice.

Siobhan smiles a big one with her eyes and that, and I know that this wedding is gonna be so live.

When I get home, I'm still picturing that smile and I dance down the hallway. I barely have time to put my stuff down in my room when Mum calls me and Adrian for dinner. She's been cooking for us a lot the last few days, making us eat together like in a gravy advert before she goes to work. Can't lie, I kinda like it; Adrian not so much.

'Do we have to do this again? Swear on my life, we don't need to be doing this. I was in the middle of a game.' Adrian comes moaning out of his room.

'Boy, come in and sit your butt down, the game will still be there after dinner.'

Me and Adrian sit down but Mum doesn't join us, she's just kinda lingering, taking tiny sips of water. She ladles our polenta and gravy and goes back to standing by the oven.

Without Mum it feels kinda weird, so I ask Adrian how his day was. He tells me to mind my own business, snitches get stitches. Mum starts telling him not to be so rude, but she's interrupted by her phone ringing. She quickly reaches out and ends the call before it even gets to two rings.

'Boys, I hope you enjoy your food. Polenta is really good for you, and it goes with anything,' she says, turning to us.

'Mum, was I born in a polenta?' I ask her.

Adrian sniggers.

Mum's baffled. 'What the hell kinda question is that?'

I tell her that I heard pregnant women all have a polenta where they keep the baby, and after they're born the baby climbs out of the polenta and starts a life on the run.

'That's placenta, hun,' Mum tells me, but she's looking back at her phone that's on the counter.

'Come on, bro, I'm eating. Can we not talk about placenta?' Adrian pushes his plate away.

'Mum, what's a prostate? And why are they so important during American elections?' Mum's phone rings again, making her jump. She snatches it and puts it on silent mode. OK, this is really weird, Mum's usually not afraid of anything; when we watched *The Conjuring 3*, she laughed at us whenever me and Adrian got shook. We tried sleeping with our lights on, but Mum turned them off and said if the electricity bill is too high, she'll be scarier than any horror film. You have no idea what it's like to check under your bed every night, not for monsters, but for your own mum who might be haunting you.

'Boys, I'm gonna go for a walk,' she says. She goes to look at her reflection in the kitchen window, but before she can, the phone rings again. This time she does a little scream and grabs her glass of water instead. She throws it on the floor and it smashes into pieces, water going everywhere. Me and Adrian just look at her, mouths open. There's some mad awkward silence when she storms out.

After a while, Adrian scrapes his placenta into the bin and goes back to his game. I'm pretty sure I can hear him ordering pizza. Mum once said that she doesn't know where he gets his money but she doesn't want to know. The screen on Mum's phone lights up; she forgot it on the counter. I glance around to make sure I'm alone, and then go over to look at the number flashing. There are four missed calls from the same number, which is saved as 'Do not pick up'. My thumb is on autopilot as I call the number back and hold the phone to my ear.

'Ms Thompson, thank you for finally returning my call,' a slow, smirking voice says. Gregory Flynn. I hang up the call and drop the phone like a hot potato. I'm running out of time.

Can't lie, this is all getting a bit much. I miss the days where life used to be easy, I could just go to school, spit some bars and then come home to eat hot wings and chips. They say that almonds are formed under pressure, but I ain't an almond. The bubble in my chest is inflating, everything feels like a lot right now. Out of ultra instinct, I pull out my phone. My thumb hovers above Karen's number. It takes me a few seconds, but I suck it up and hit the call sign. I hope she answers – she told me she'd call back if I leave a message. It's ringing, and I cross my fingers, shoulders, knees and toes. Please pick up, please pick up. I'm about to give up, but I feel hella relieved when I hear her say . . .

'Hello?'

'Yo, Karen, it's Growls, what you saying?' I don't make a lot of phone calls, I'm not BT or 999.

Karen sounds like she's somewhere busy, and I hear her moving to somewhere quieter.

'Growls, what can I do for you, is everything alright?' Even over the phone she's so polite she's the kind of person who would take the dry piece of chicken from Morley's without complaining. I don't know where to start, but I'm remembering Gregory Flynn's horrible voice in my head, and I just start telling her everything. I'm not sure if I should be chatting about this with her, I don't want to air my mum's business or nothing, but Karen told me to be open and honest. It's harder than it looks.

'Well, we're definitely getting evicted, me and my mum and my brother.' I tell her about what happened in the kitchen earlier, how my mum freaked out, and it was him calling her and setting her on edge. 'So yeah, my mum is shook, I'm shook too, and I'll never see my friends again. MC Squared will have to split up, and Siobhan is like that one song on my playlist that I love and could listen to all the time. And now I have to leave everything behind?' All the words come falling out my mouth. The scratchy feeling in my throat is back, that chest balloon that pushes out the tears is growing.

'I don't wanna go, Karen. I really don't wanna leave the ends, I wanna stay in my house.' My face is proper leaking, like leak and potato soup. 'I've been trying and trying to find a solution, but it just ain't coming. My brain wasn't clever enough, and now my mum's tired from working so much, and my family's gonna be homeless.' I'm bare sniffling. 'How am I supposed to be a hero like you said when I can't do anything right?' I'm a mess.

Karen makes that sound people do when they have no answers and can't help. It makes things even worse because she's supposed to always have the answers. I just sit here crying like I'm watching one of those emotional Christmas adverts. I need Karen to say something.

'Hey, even heroes need saving sometimes. You're allowed to let people be there for you,' Karen finally says. 'I can try to speak to the tenant management organisation? I'm sure they'll do everything they can to help.' They won't do nothing. Karen don't realise that people on the block mean nothing to these jerks in glasses and clipboards. Things don't work the same in these ends like they do other places. Adrian's been stop-and-searched four times this year, these people ain't in it to help us. I tell Karen thanks, but I know I've already lost. It's curtains.

'Listen, Growls, I'm going to tell you two things, and I want you to pay very close attention to what I'm saying.' Her voice is less playful than usual. 'Firstly, you *can't* predict what's going to happen in life, you just can't. The things you're scared will happen might not happen, and things you're not expecting will hit you like a tonne of bricks. The only certainty in this world is that nothing is certain.' I stop crying and blow my nose before she goes on. 'Life is too unpredictable to be motivated by fear of things that have not happened.'

'But, Karen, this *is* happening, and it's happening to me right now.' I know I shouldn't be scared, but I don't want her to give me Paul's hope.

'I think you mean "false hope", and the point still stands. If you're constantly afraid of the future, you're missing out on the present. And the other thing I wanted to tell you is just as important. When I was just a bit older than you, my dad was diagnosed with leukaemia, a type of cancer.' Oh damn, this is getting deep. 'Now originally I was terrified of what was going to happen, a little like you. But when he started deteriorating and was given only a few months to live, that fear had to go, because there was nothing I could do to change it. I spent every moment with him that I could, being with him, loving him, because I knew that every day could be the last day that I had with him.' I can hear Karen's voice change, it's more nasal, but she's not proper crying, not like me. 'If this really is the last time you'll see your friends, which I'm pretty certain it's not, you go out there and you be with them, enjoy them, support them, and spend every moment you can with the people you love. Growls, the ability to love is a glorious thing, and to live in fear takes you away from that.' We both stay silent for a moment.

'I just feel like such a failure.' How did it get to this point? I'm crying down the phone to a grown lady who's not even family.

'You're not a failure, Growls. I know for a fact that you're not a failure,' Karen says. I wipe the water from my eyes.

'How do you know?'

'Because, Growls, you *called* me. And you are telling me how you feel. You are more open and honest than that first day when you first came into my office and lay down like a mermaid.' We both laugh a little bit at the thought. 'You've made such strides since we started, and you should be incredibly proud of yourself.' She pauses for a moment. 'Relationships are like house plants in a way, if you keep nurturing them, they'll never die.' We do some breathing exercises together, and it does make me feel much better. I'm light again, like cream in a can. 'Do you have any questions or anything else to say?'

Nah, I'm cool, I think I get it.

'Good.' She says. 'Now go be a superhero.'

20

Laughter Is the Best Medicine (Except for Real Medicine)

I texted Shanks last night to ask if I could come visit him. Siobhan called me from her stupid landline to check if I'd done it yet, and she refused to hang up the phone until the message was sent. He responded straight away, saying he was going to ask his mum. Then he replied ten minutes later to say that she said yes, I can come over tomorrow, and he's super excited to see me.

Not gonna lie, I always thought that seeing Shanks would be the best thing in the world to me, and it is, but it's also making me feel a bit sick, I don't know how things will go down. What if he's vexed that I would do Raptology without him? What if this is the end of MC Squared and our solo careers send us into a meltdown like the ice caps in global warming? What if 'ice caps' is what Ice Cube calls his headwear and he rides an icicle on his ice-capades? Maybe I'm overthinking this.

This morning I set my alarm for nine o'clock, but I've been awake since seven. I read the text message again to make triple sure that I'm not gonna be late.

Mum offered to come with, but I know she's tired since her cleaning shifts got longer. Sunday mornings are pretty calm anyway. Adrian has football training, and I usually just scroll on my phone until lunchtime. When you're lying down and scrolling on your phone and you hate dropping it on your face, you can lie down *over* the phone and let gravity do all the work instead #lifehack.

Today's different though. I've already scrolled on my phone and showered and now I'm pouring myself breakfast. I'm careful to only use a tiny bit of milk on my cereal, Mum likes saving money on milk. It's bare dry though, feels like it's thirsting to death, which would make my breakfast a cereal killer.

I keep looking at the clock, I can't take my mind off seeing Shanks, I think I just need to leave already.

I can do this. I can go be there for my boy. I can ask Shanks' permission to do Raptology solo, and even if he says no then he's still my best friend. As I'm leaving yard, I feel light-headed and heavy-headed at the same time.

Shanks' mum opens the door, but she doesn't let me in

straight away. She looks like she hasn't smiled in a minute, the wrinkles around her mouth are pointing downwards. She tells me to 'be careful with him', as if he's a daisy chain or a really heavy birthday cake or something. I nod along, because answering back to a Caribbean mum is like twerking on a grizzly bear. It can be done, technically, but it'll be brief. She stares me down for a couple more seconds, and then stands aside to let me in. That's what I thought, shook one. I tiptoe past her and quickly run upstairs to Shanks' room. I can feel her eyes still on me, like when you accidentally walk into a spider's web and it gets caught around your head, and you have to scream a little bit and run and claw at your own face like a demon.

Shanks is lying in bed watching something on his laptop as I walk into his room. He doesn't look much different, except his fade has grown out and he looks tired like a grown-up. He sits up and closes the laptop.

'Bro,' he says.

I can't help it, I just start crying. 'Allow you being gone, I missed you, my G.' I'm really crying now and my voice is shaking. I tell him that school is no fun without him and that I don't play FIFA any more and I miss him so much it hurts sometimes. He closes his eyes and leans his head back on the pillow.

'I know, I missed you too, my guy.'

'I don't get it. What happened to you?' I ask him. He

looks down, and doesn't say anything. Then I see him start blinking because his eyes are filling up too. 'Hey, you don't have to tell me anything if you don't want to.' I don't want to see him upset. Not now, not ever.

He doesn't look up. 'What happened was . . . The thing is . . . I know it sounds strange, but I just got really tired.' I don't know what he means. 'Growls, after we went live that day, I was getting the maddest messages. I got anxious.' Anxious? 'Yeah, I stopped eating, my mum was cooking everything, oxtail, pizza, everything, but my appetite was gone. I can't explain it, I just couldn't eat anything. And then sometimes, when I would leave the house, I'd feel this thing in my chest, like it was tight and it was strangling me from the inside.' Damn, even the needles bubble I sometimes get sounds easier than dealing with what Shanks has been feeling. It actually sounds hella peak. 'It was,' he sniffs. 'I had this thing called an anxiety attack. It's kinda like a fake heart attack.'

'Like when you drop your phone?' I ask.

'Worse,' he says, 'and it got so bad. I tried to hide it from everyone, but my parents clocked. I didn't eat or sleep for three days, and that's when I went to hospital.' He closes his eyes and shakes his head. He's still picturing the whole thing. 'The doctors kept saying it was stress and fatigue that was causing the anxiety. When I came out, I couldn't leave the house. I knew that everyone would laugh at me, or worse.'

'Cry at you?'

'Nah, that's stupid, man, come on. But yeah, I was having these anxiety attacks every time I tried to leave the house. After that, my parents went on demon time. They took away my phone, they blocked almost everything on the internet, and they started bringing me work from school so that I didn't have to go in. I couldn't even jump on FIFA because I was getting messages there as well, and it would trigger the anxiety. Basically, they did everything they could for me to rest up. That's why you couldn't visit until now. I know you're my boy, but I needed to get better. Fully.' He finally looks up at me.

'I didn't know any of that.' Of course he was gonna hurt, he cares about people and what they think. I put my head in my hands. I should've known, I can't believe I've been so stupid.

'Growls, you're not stupid for not knowing things that I didn't tell you. It wasn't your fault,' he says.

When I hear that, the weight in my chest gets really heavy, pulling me down on the inside. 'Bro, it was though. All of this. I didn't even tell you *why* I went live that day.' He looks confused, like he's about to say something, but I have to tell him before I bottle it. 'I wanted to impress Tanisha. I wanted her to like me so bad I wasn't thinking, I had no idea.' I close my eyes and brace myself. He deserves to shout at me, or even take a swing. But he doesn't, he just lies back. His face is a blank emotion. I'm such an idiot.

I messed everything up for a girl who took three years to learn my name. Siobhan learned my name straight away.

'Look, Shanks, I'm sorry. I'm really, really sorry, I didn't want any of this to happen.' He's the star of the show and Tanisha only had a cameo. If I wasn't so obsessed with being liked by someone who don't like me, the friend I love wouldn't be here, locked away in his room. My hands cover my eyes and I shake my head, I can't believe this.

Shanks stays silent for a while. 'Growls. *You* didn't send me those messages.'

I stop shaking my head. I still can't say anything, though.

'You made a mistake. Whatever reason you had, you're not the one that put me here. Thanks for apologising. What you did was really dumb, but you didn't make people at school react the way they did.' I can't help but stand up and hug him. The weight in my chest gets a bit lighter and I feel like I'm breathing normal for the first time in ages. I'm still sorry though, I was so selfish before.

'If you were before, I think you're less selfish now. Look at you, doing therapy, phone calls, cooking with your mum, I feel like you've really grown up these past few weeks.' He says it bare sincerely like the host of a nature documentary. Have I grown? In the mirror I look the same. I guess I just have to keep doing what Karen said, be there for the people I care about.

'Speaking of people you care about . . .' Shanks starts

fluttering his eyelashes and making kissing noises. 'How's Siobhan?' Don't watch that, even hearing her name makes my mouth smile like I'm at a concert on a summer's eve. If it wasn't for Siobhan, I probably would've been too scared to visit Shanks today. She's so cool. I tell Shanks that Siobhan is homeschooled too, so they have something in common already.

'I wanna meet her. Now that my appetite's back and I'm sleeping normally, I should be out and about in the next couple weeks. We'll be able to hang out all summer and the three of us can shoot hoops and play FIFA every day.'

'Yeah, about that . . .' I weren't gonna go *in* like that, but I start telling him about the eviction, about Gregory Flynn, and about Mum's phone and all the letters, and about how I'm scared. Like, for real scared, because I don't wanna leave ends, I don't want Mum and Adrian to be to be homeless, I've only just got Shanks back, I've met Siobhan, and school isn't even that mad any more. This guy is bare animated, gasping and covering his mouth and nodding and sighing while I talk. The thought of losing everything makes my stomach drop like an apple pie on William Shakespeare's head #gravity, but in the worst way.

'Growls,' he says, 'what are you gonna do? You have to have a plan, you always have a plan. Remember when Mrs O'Riley said she was going to call your mum, and you pretended to cry so that she would let you off?'

'Pretended to cry. Yeah, that's right, I was pretending. It one hundred per cent wasn't real tears or nothing.'

'That's what I'm saying, you always think of something. Or that time you fully pretended to pee your pants in the cinema because you wanted your money back for the ticket.'

'Pretended. Yeah. The film wasn't even scary. Hey, let's stop talking about things I pretended to do.' It's time to talk about something else. Raptology is on the tip of my tongue. I take a deep breath, this is it. You got this. 'I actually need to ask you something, and I get it if you say no because we were supposed to do it together, but it's the only thing I can think of to save my house.'

'Anything.' He's proper eager. I can't look at him in the eye when I ask what I'm about to ask.

'I don't wanna force nothing, but Raptology is coming up. There's prize money that could help us keep the yard if I win. This could be a redemption story for MC Squared.' If he says no, then it's calm, he's still my guy.

Shanks bites his lip, like he's thinking, but he shakes his head slowly. 'Bruv, that sounds decent, but Imma have to let you down, I'm sorry. It's not for me, not any more, not now. And besides, I agreed with my mum and dad that I'd be chilling off at home for the next few weeks.' I can respect that. My guy needs to rest. 'Sorry, Growls, even if I wanted to, I'm just not ready for a massive crowd like that.'

Can't lie, I ain't gonna pretend like it doesn't hurt, but

Shanks comes first. Always. 'You do what you need to do, man. If you need to be home, then I'll back it. And I rate you for being honest.'

'You should do it solo though,' he says. 'Just because I can't be there, doesn't mean you shouldn't.'

'Really?' My heart just leaped like a gazelle.

'Growls, if it'll help save your yard and keep you in ends, you totally have to do this. I think you might actually have a chance of winning this thing.' My head is floating and my chest feels like singing. This guy is my OG, I'm never going to forget that. And trust me, I forget lots of things.

'Seriously, bro,' I tell him, 'you don't know how grateful I am that you're so chill about this.'

Shanks looks down, biting his lip again. I can tell he has something serious to say. 'Yeah, the thing is –' he looks up at the ceiling now – 'like, rapping is fun, but it was always more of your thing. I was just happy to do it with you because it gave us a reason to hang out.'

He . . . he what? I let the words sink in. Did he ever like rapping?

'Not really, but I never wanted to say, I didn't want us to stop chilling together.' How could he ever think I would stop chilling with him because of that? Shanks is the type of friend that becomes family. We don't need to do all the same stuff all the time for that to still be true.

'Shanks, we were friends before MC Squared, and you'll

always be my brother whatever happens. Hey, if Julius Caesar Salad and Napoleon stayed friends after they took over the world, then so can we.'

Shanks smiles now and perks up.

'They weren't friends, they were years apart.'

'Erm, no, Napoleon was bone apart. See, this is why I miss you, bro, I love our historical discussions. I don't miss you because we rap, I miss you because you're my OG for life.'

We hug it out, and now I can't wait to go home and tell Siobhan.

We spend some time talking about what Shanks has been doing in his free time. He's allowed on the internet again, now that his parents have blocked a bunch of pages, and he spends a lot of time watching documentaries. He's telling me about one where ants use a pharaoh moan to communicate, even though they're not Egyptian.

'No, it's called a *pheromone*, it's about smell, and humans have it too,' he says.

'Wait, so I can communicate with ants? I knew it! Remember when they kept crawling on me at night? I must have been summoning them.'

'Nah, bro, it's because you were putting sugar under your pillow.' Shanks always said it was a bad idea.

'Adrian told me it would give me sweet dreams.' It was peak, and the ants got worse when I tried spreading strawberry jam on my sheets. Mum started wilin' out when I told her it was a bedspread.

I love this: me and Shanks reminiscing (with a silent 'c' – thanks, Mr Rix) and laughing and chatting. Then I look up and see his mum standing in the doorway. She's smiling at us, and I have no idea how long she's been standing there. She's still smiling as she walks away.

When Shanks' dad gets back from work, we all play a card game called 'go fish'. I never get to play card games. Adrian tried a magic trick on me one time where I had to pick a card, any card, and then he'd fart in my lap. After that I started avoiding cards. Playing go fish with Shanks' fam is proper fun though, except when his mum keeps happy crying every time she looks at him.

As I'm leaving to go home an hour later, she gives me a big hug and thanks me for coming over. Wow, she's never thanked me for coming over before, which is jokes because she's thanked me for leaving plenty of times. When I hug her back, it's a bit different to hugging my mum; Shanks' mum is taller, more bony and her perfume smells sweeter. Man spent bills on that scent, that's for sure.

Life is so sick. One minute you're pooping in a dark toilet like the Batcave and the next minute you're visiting your boy and he's gonna pull through. I'm so happy I got to see him I almost forget about the fact that now Raptology is back on, there's only a couple of weeks for me to get ready. I play my hip-hop playlist on the bus back for inspiration. I been paying more attention to the lyrics and beat instead of imagining myself as a celebrity. I'm tryna pick up different flows from the rappers in my headphones, connecting lyrics to be more acrobatic than just rhyming the last word. Mr Rix was right – music is music and that's nothing to do with being famous, I'll show that at Raptology. I'd rather spit bars and not be famous than be famous for doing nothing. I don't need to be a rapper to have friends and feel useful, not when Shanks has my back and Siobhan smiles at me the way she does. The best songs are the ones that remind me of my friends, because they're the ones that make me feel six feet two inches tall. Fam, I got friends, I got family, I got Raptology, and I got lyrics for days. Feels nice to not be holding an 'L' for a change.

When I get home, I can hear Mum making food in the kitchen. I run in and give her a big hug. She looks surprised and she chuckles a little bit when she hugs me back. She asks me if I had a good day. I nod, but I don't release the hug. She asks me if everything was OK with Shanks, and I nod again. My mum doesn't deserve to be kicked out into the street. She should be living in a nice big house, playing card games with me and Adrian.

Summer You Win and Summer You Lose

It's the last day of school and everyone's buzzing because we get to wear our own clothes. Can't lie, my drip is on point. I'm wearing my Air Max that Adrian bought online from some American shop, but he gave them to me because they spelled 'Max' wrong. They spelled it 'Macks', which makes sense because potato-tomato.

I go to find Mr Rix and say goodbye and thanks for chilling with me after Shanks left. He's not in his classroom so Imma just wait for him until he gets back. He's taking a while, so I get up and walk around. I stand by the window and look out at the tree. It reminds me about what he said, that things are perfect because they're not perfect. It kinda puts me at ease. The door bangs open and he looks happily surprised to find me standing there.

'Shaun, hi, I wasn't expecting to see you. How are you?'
This guy is always so jolly, he's like an auntie with shopping
running for a bus that's stopped just long enough for her
to make it on.

'Yeah, I'm good, sir, I just wanted to say thanks for helping
me.' I'm looking down at my shoes when I say it, but he
still seems happy.

'You are most welcome. And how are things at home?'

'Yeah, they're aite,' I say. 'I'm doing Raptology.' I blurt
out. I start telling him about the competition and how
Shanks gave me permission to do it alone. 'And I get what
you mean about spitting bars to have fun. I don't need to
come for other rappers in my lyrics, I think if my bars good
enough then I won't have to. I didn't really acknowledge
for the longest, but I guess I'm a tree as well. You did bits for
me, and I rate that, so thank you.'

'I am very, very proud of you, Shaun.' He claps his hands
and rubs them together with excitement. 'May I offer some
additional advice for your competition?' I nod. 'Be different.
You don't have to copy everyone else, you can tell your
own story. And what a story you have to tell. Now if you'll
excuse me, I have to go and squeeze eight weeks of marking
into a six-week holiday. Hopefully there'll be time for at
least a few days in the sun.'

When he shakes my hand to say goodbye, it's actually a
bit sad. He's taught me a lot this year.

'Come on, you can do better than that. Firm your grip, employers are going to want a strong, confident handshake.' We do it again. 'Better.' He smiles.

Can't lie, as I leave the school for the last time until September, I feel hella relieved. I finally made it. I spot Tanisha and her friends across the road, and it feels like so long ago that I had a crush on her. We kinda give each other major side-eye, before going back to ignoring each other like two divorced parents at a school play. I can't believe that for almost a whole year the only thing I wanted to do was braid her hair at the beach, but those days are long gone silver.

After school, Mum wants me to pop to the shops to buy milk; she only gave me enough for a small bottle because she don't get paid until Tuesday. I'm lining up to pay, and the guy in front of me is taking long. He's got this really slow, nasal voice as he's asking for stuff. It sounds familiar.

Suddenly my stomach goes cold and my whole body stiffens as he turns to leave. It's Gregory Flynn, standing here in my shop. He pauses when he notices me and does that horrible smile that bad guys do in films before a madness happens. It's like he can see straight through my soul. I drop the milk, and it bursts on the floor. As I'm running out Mr Ravi is shouting stuff, but Gregory Fynn doesn't move. He just stands there smirking.

I'm out of breath when I get home. I don't wanna tell Mum that I saw Gregory Flynn in the shop, but thankfully she doesn't get too mad about the milk. There's no point crying over spilled milk, unless it spills in your eye, I guess. My heart is still beating fast though, so I try to breathe in and out, like with Karen, and think about something positive. The school year is finally over. By the time I go back in September, I'll have a deep voice like Terry Crews and probably a body like Terry Crews and a proper defined jawline like – you guessed it – Gabriel Union. When I catch myself in the mirror, I see that I'm more like Beyoncé. I don't have her dance moves though. Or maybe I do . . .

I start twerking in the reflection, just to see what it looks like. My twerkathon accelerates, I'm picturing a space-hopper race between my thighs. I look too happy so I put on my serious face, like I'm a fierce diva or a grumpy cat. I'm in the zone now, throwing my bunda up and down like a yo-yo. It's taken over, it has a mind of its own. Hold tight, these cakes have gone nuclear. Crashing my glutes like invisible whackamole . . .

My phone starts ringing. It's Siobhan.

'Hey, what you up to?' she says.

'Nothing weird,' I reply.

'Erm, OK. Yeah, I was just calling to remind you that the wedding is on Saturday, if you're still up for it.' She sounds a bit nervous. I wanna tell her that I'd rather eat my own face than miss a chance to spend time with her.

'Yeah, Saturday, I think I'm still free. I was supposed to be getting my black belt in origami, but that can always wait.'

'Cool. Right, let's meet at the church at 10.30? It's at Our Lady of Sorrows near Old Kent Road.' She then asks me to wear a suit, and I know she ain't talking about my Batman costume that I got for Christmas a few years ago.

'I think my brother has one from my nan's funeral. I just wore my school trousers and a shirt.' Mum was on a budget.

'Great. So, I guess I'll see you on Saturday. I'm really looking forward to it. Oh, and by the way, origami isn't a martial art.'

'Yes, it is.' How dare she.

'No, it really isn't.' OK, fine, I fold. She's so cool.

22

Wedding Day: Part One — I Take Thee, Thy Though

'Mum, Adrian's suit is too big, all three of us could fit into this outfit at the same time.' It's wedding day and this morning has been so stressful. Siobhan wants to me to be at the church early so we can go in together, and I'm still not ready to leave. The suit is massive, I look like a female newsreader from the 1980s. I tried to spice it up by wearing a tank top underneath instead of a shirt, but Adrian and Mum both laughed and threw popcorn at me. Imma just have to wear my school shirt.

I try three different pairs of shoes but end up throwing them all across the room because they don't match with my on somble. Mum wants me to wear these dead, grandaddy shoes with skinny laces that Adrian wore to my cousin's christening, but they're the worst things I've ever seen in my life. Seriously, I'd rather wear purple crocs #footfashionfelony #holycrocomoly. In the end, I just go in Adrian's old Vans that are still a little big and make me feel like a clown or a scuba diver. I barely have time for breakfast before I have to leave to make it in time.

'You look so handsome,' Mum says. 'Come over here so Mummy can give you a kiss.' Erm, no thanks #ichooselife. She's standing in her dressing gown, sipping on tea. Adrian pretends to be sick into his cornflakes.

Just before I leave the house I put on an old tie that must've been my dad's. I tie it in two loops, under, over and tuck, just like Mr Rix taught me. It takes me two or three goes to get it perfect and Mum helps me adjust it. She kisses me on the forehead, all gentle, like she's kissing a newborn, and tells me to have fun. Can't lie, today's gonna be a mad one, I can feel it.

You can't steal it,
Thought I was done with the freestyles but they're green lit.
Like the hulk onstage, did a press-up got my bulk on rage,
And now it's strange, I mean it.

Don't watch that. The king of the underground is back.

Fam, I hate being on the bus. People on the top deck keep turning round to look at me coz I forgot my headphones so I have to play Shaggy through the speakers on my phone.

They don't know that it's the only thing that helps me relax, I know all the words and everything.

When I make my way down the stairs and stumble over to the exit door, I see Siobhan standing there, waiting to get off. My heart jumps into my throat.

'Oh my days, we been on the same bus the whole time!' My voice is bare excited.

'No way,' she says. 'I was actually going to sit upstairs too, but some fool was playing his music out loud.'

'It wasn't me.'

We get off the bus and the church is two minutes away. I took screenshots of Google Maps when I was at home because I don't have data. Now that I can see her properly in the daylight, Siobhan looks so different. Her red hair is tied up and I can see her neck. And her shoulders, knees and toes. For real, I need to not stare too much. Even her face looks a little different.

'Where did your freckles go?' I ask her.

Siobhan blushes. 'You can't see them because I'm wearing make-up. Does it look weird? It does, doesn't it? I look weird.'

'I don't think you look weird. With or without make-up, you're still bare pretty. Like the girl rabbit from *Space Jam*.' It's true, she's so beautiful and amazing and fierce, when she looks at you, you can't help but be amazed. I can see why the other Looney Toons in the Toon Squad look up to her.

As we get closer to the church, I see more and more

people rocking up. Guys in suits and women with really big hats that block the sunlight from their faces. I can tell that Siobhan is feeling awkward, mainly because she's gone bright red and also because she keeps telling me she's feeling awkward. A couple of people smile and nod at her, then look at me a bit confused when they clock that we're together.

'Just ignore them, I always do,' Siobhan says as we go into the church. That makes me feel a tiny bit better. Yo, this place is massive. The ceilings are even higher than the ones in the National Gallery, you could fit a whole council block in here. And the place is covered in flowers, from top to bottom. Every colour and size I can think of, all over the shop, and there are millions of petals scattered down the aisle. If Mr Rix thinks trees are beautiful, he'd wet himself if he saw this. I spot a guy on a balcony above us, he's taking photos with one of those real cameras, not even on his phone. It's the FBI. They're here. They finally found us.

'That's not the FBI,' Siobhan laughs. 'That's my cousin Jack. He's the wedding photographer.'

'Oh, cool.' I can relax. 'What does the wedding photographer do?'

'He takes photos of the wedding.'

'Right.' I guess that adds up. I hope he captures my good side. Because we all have a dark side. A troubled past.

'What are you on about? You're so random.' She properly laughs at my nonsense. And that makes me smile too.

More and more people are entering the church. We're sitting on the groom's side. It makes me wonder about gay weddings, which side do people sit on? Siobhan tells me they sit on whoever's side of the family they are. That makes sense, it also explains why family members can't marry each other, too much panic about where to sit. I heard Queen Elizabeth married her second cousin, that's probably why they called her Elizabeth the Second.

I think the wedding's gonna start soon. Siobhan checks her watch and confirms. She's so grown-up, checking her watch. All of a sudden the organ starts playing, so I start skanking in slow-motion, my hands reaching up, cutting shapes, and my head doing a gentle robot pop, left and right. I only stop when Siobhan gives me a look and people are concentrating on me instead of the bride arriving at the back of the church. There's a gasp and some chatter as she starts coming down the aisle. Aisle be back, lol. Siobhan shakes her head at that one. Some of the large hats are crying when they see her come through, it's not even that deep. The bride's dress is kinda lit though, it's pure white like the Oscars. It's too long though, so there's a couple bridesmaids making sure it don't scrape along the floor too much. I can't even see her shoes.

The groom is waiting at the front, looking nervous like he's at a self-check out and there's people waiting behind him. The bride and her dad reach the altar, and the whole church goes silent as the priest starts his ting, talking about 'dearly beloved' like he's the one getting married.

Bruh, time is going by proper slow. It feels like this has been going on for around five hours, but when I look at Siobhan's watch I clock it's only been fifteen minutes. To pass the time, me and Siobhan play 'rock paper scissors'. Then we have a staring contest, but I lose because I get embarrassed when I see how green and beautiful her eyes are looking. When it comes time where the priest says, 'Speak now or forever hold your peace,' I'm looking around the room to spot the person who stands up and shouts, 'I object!' but it doesn't happen. I guess I'll have to wait for another wedding.

When the Mass finally ends, like a Brazilian years later, I feel my stomach rumbling like a thunderstorm in the Atlantic. We walk out the church to wait by the doors and the entire crowd starts gathering.

Wow, people are actually throwing rice out here. Mum would never tolerate this, she'd call it a massive waste of food and get me and Adrian to sweep it up into a little jar. At my wedding I'm gonna ask people to throw chips at me. At least if I catch some of them, I can save some P by feeding it to people at the reception. I do low-key think the world would be safer if we threw rice at each other instead of using guns and that. Imagine if Abraham Lincoln didn't get shot, he just had rice thrown on him in a drive-by rice attack. He'd still be alive today.

23

Wedding Day: Part Two — Wear Thor Out There, Romeo

Thank God we're at the same table. I see 'Siobhan' and 'Siobhan's guest' next to each other on the big whiteboard at the reception. We're in a community hall in Fenway Estate which is on the 78 to Liverpool Street. I know that because London is my home, gang-gang, but mainly because I once fell asleep on the bus and woke up there.

All day people been coming up to Siobhan, asking how her mum is and basically ignoring me. I didn't clock, but Siobhan gets proper weird when people ask about her mum. She gives me a side-look and answers in a quiet voice, or she brushes them off and drags me away. I guess it's calm if people ignore me because they don't really know who I am, but there's a look in their eyes when they see me, the same look a librarian has when I come in to use their public toilets.

Jack the wedding photographer is cool though, he takes a few minutes to come chat to us. He asks me my name and who I am and that. Introductions are always hella awkward, I never know if I should shake hands or bump fists or stand there silently winking at each other. After a while I stop winking and he awkwardly turns to Siobhan and asks about her mum. She makes the same awkward face and I can tell she's blushing, like a child putting money in the hat of a street performer, or an office worker who made eye contact with a window cleaner on the seventh floor.

'Yeah, she's good, thanks,' Siobhan says, looking at me and then looking at her feet.

'Good, good. How are you guys coping?' Jack asks.

Siobhan is giving him a strained look. Like her brain is telling him to stop talking. 'Yeah, we're fine, Jack. Mum's good and I'm good. Anyway, we're going to find our seats now. But we'll catch up with you later. I'm sure you've got lots of pictures to take, the bride will be here soon.' Jack nods and shakes my hand before he disappears into the crowd.

Can't lie, when me and Siobhan finally sit down we're both a little relieved to get a rest from people. 'Look, I'm really sorry, I wasn't expecting this wedding to be so dead. I really thought this would be fun. I'm so stupid, these things are never fun. Listen, if you want to go, save yourself, I don't blame you.' She looks like she's about to cry. Allow seeing her upset, Siobhan is usually the brave one out of me and her. Legit she's like a superhero, and like Karen said, even heroes need saving sometimes. All I have to do is be here.

'I don't want to go,' I tell her.

She looks up, her eyes are kinda hopeful. 'You don't?' she says, smiling. My favourite smile.

'Skeen, of course not. I wanna be wherever you are.' If Siobhan was trapped down a well well well, I wouldn't even mind being trapped with her. Like, I'd rather we weren't trapped, but I'm saying I wouldn't mind. We could just hug and listen to music until we're rescued.

She looks up at me, and her hand starts to reach for mine. It's getting closer and closer. My heart is beating bare fast. I'm not holding anything, so she must be reaching just to hold it. Oh my days, what if my palms are too sweaty? She'll think I just licked my hand for no reason, which I obviously don't do any more. My days, this is it. As I start to feel her skin touch mine, someone sits down at our table and she quickly withdraws her hand. Now my heart just hurts, and I want everyone to leave so we can recapture the moment. But guests are starting to take their places and chatter in the hall gets louder and louder. We're at the teenagers' table, which is cool because the adult table looks boring as hell and the kids' table is full of posers.

A couple of the people sitting with us are Siobhan's cousins, the rest of them aren't. Everyone just says a shy 'hello' and immediately goes on their phones when they sit down. Can't lie, if Siobhan wasn't here I'd probably do the same.

'Now you see why I'm not upset that I don't have one,' Siobhan says, all smug.

The entire hall stands up and starts applauding when the bride and groom enter. Jack is flashing away with his camera, and people cheer even louder when they start kissing. Everyone's standing up applauding for so long that my legs get tired and I start to sit down, but Siobhan gives me a look and shakes her head as if to say it's a bad idea.

The newly-weds finally sit down at the main table, which means we don't have to stand any more. Fam, I ain't stood for that long since that week where I sat on a cactus and my gluteus maximus felt like it had broken glass in it.

'Why did you sit on a cactus?' Siobhan asks.

'Because if I didn't, Shanks would have sat on it by accident.'

'Why would Shanks sit on it?'

'Because I accidentally spat chilli in his eye.'

'I have so many follow-up questions to what you just said,' she says. Bruv, she's saying it like it's confusing or something. 'It *is* confusing,' she insists.

'No, it's not,' I tell her. 'Taxes are confusing. Recipes are confusing. Things like Brexit and shirts with left-handed buttons are confusing.'

'Spitting chilli in your best friend's eye and sitting on a cactus is also a little confusing,' she insists. We go back and forth until we notice someone standing beside us. It's a grown-up, kinda hench, and he looks like he plays rugby, not badminton or clarinet. He has red hair too.

'Hi, Siobhan,' he says, his voice is bare Irish. He sounds like Roy Keane from *Match of the Day*. 'How's your ma, are you two doing OK?'

'We're doing fine,' Siobhan replies. She turns to face me again, ignoring him like he's a vegan vampire with no teeth and a desire for celery. He kinda glances at me quickly and does a half-smile before putting his hand on her shoulder. I see her tense up a little, and for a second I feel like she's about to slap his hand away. But she firms it until he gets the message and walks away. And that's when I get it, that look in his eyes when he looked at Siobhan, the same look everyone here's been giving her, it's pity. People been looking at me like that my whole life. They feel sorry for her.

I kinda wanna talk to Siobhan about it, but we get distracted when the food starts coming out. Bruv, this is some tiny portion. It's ravioli but there's ravi-only three pieces of it. That joke was fire, don't watch that. Siobhan's not laughing but I know Shanks would appreciate it. The ravioli ration's in the middle of the plate with a thin line of white sauce and some *Toy Story* sized bits of lettuce on the side. Damn, I knew we shouldn't have wasted all that rice by throwing it outside the church. Now I'm gonna starve to death at a wedding.

'You're not going to starve, this is just the entrée.' Siobhan laughs, back to her normal self again. 'It's like an appetizer.'

'I thought we came in through the entrée. And appetizers are just baby portions of lies that rich people tell their stomachs. If they were normal-sized, they'd just be a meal.' It's cool though, there's no one sitting at that empty space across the table so Imma just take their tiny appetizers of dishonesty. I walk around to borrow the food from whoever didn't turn up. The other kids watch, and one girl even shakes her head, but I don't care; I'm so hungry I could ride a horse.

'Oh my God, you are so embarrassing,' Siobhan says, covering her face.

'You wanna share?' I ask her.

She thinks about it for a sec. 'Yeah, I'm hungry too.' Then she mimics my voice to make it deeper. 'Or as you would say, "Yeah, I'm hungry, still."' Lol it's actually a pretty good impression. We both pick at the ravioli, but because it's in one bowl our faces are proper close. I can count her eye lashes. There's at least four.

'Surely I have more than four eyelashes.' She flutters them, looking bare pretty.

'I said *at least* four,' I repeat. She's smiling and I can't help it, I'm smiling back. She's been there for me since day, and I want her to know that we can talk about literally anything. I low-key wanna ask her about the weird energy when people are chatting to her, but I don't know how. We never get to talk about Siobhan and how she's feeling, it feels like we only ever talk about . . . me. And after being with Shanks the other day, I know that I can do this, that sometimes all I have to do is listen. Just as I go to tell her that, one of the caterers comes out from behind us and puts a bottle of wine on the table. Siobhan stops smiling and her face is suddenly wide with panic.

'Excuse me, we don't want that at our table. Excuse me!' She's calling out, but the guy doesn't hear and has already walked off. Her eyes are bare open and she's grabbed onto my hand but not in the romantic way like I wanted before, she's squeezing it kinda tight. I've never seen her like this. Bruv, this must be some low-quality wine, not that I would know. Mum always told me that wine is the undoing of men. And if it undoes men, imagine what it could do to a kid like me.

Siobhan's had enough. She breaks out of her trance and backs her chair up, pushing away from the table. She tells me she wants to go thank the bride and groom for inviting her to the wedding, but I think it's just an excuse to get away from the wine. As we stand up to go over, I spot one of her cousins reaching for the bottle to pour himself a drink. I wait for Siobhan to walk a bit ahead, and I quickly grab the bottle before her cousin can take it. If Siobhan doesn't want this at the table then I'll put it somewhere else. I got her back. I carry it in my hand as I join Siobhan just as she's approaching the main table. She's saying hello to her uncle, the groom. I bend down to pretend to tie my shoelace and leave the bottle on the floor; thankfully no one clocks me as I stand up straight. Siobhan once told me off for littering because she said it was inconsiderate and disgusting. I agree, but it's not littering if I do it indoors, it's more of an entrée.

Siobhan's uncle smiles and stands up to give Siobhan a hug. The bride doesn't, she just does some little weird smile where her mouth moves but her eyes don't.

'Thanks for coming,' the bride says. 'And we're so glad you brought a . . . friend.' Yo, I don't like the way she said that. Why the long pause? I don't know if my brain is playing tricks on my mind, but I swear she looked me up and down before she said it too.

Siobhan and her uncle are chatting away, but me and the bride stay silent. The mood quickly changes when Siobhan's uncle mentions her mum. She folds her arms and does that thing with her lips where they go inwards. I could see this coming a mile off, it's been happening all day. I'm like one of those psychics who uses the internet to predict news events only three hours after they happen.

'I'm just saying, it's too much responsibility for a girl your age to be going through all that,' the groom says. 'What about your education or your future? You need help. I don't want you screwing things up for yourself and running around the streets in a few years, doing God knows what with God knows who.' His eyes quickly look at me when he says that last bit, and the bride is sitting there nodding along. That's peak, I don't just run around in the streets, I go to art galleries and Costa now. I even remembered the silent 'P' in 'psychics'. I don't like this couple, and I especially don't like the way they're upsetting my best friend. Siobhan's not having it though. If there's one thing she can do, it's stand up for herself, even if it's against grown-ups.

'I need help? Well, I don't see anyone here lifting a finger to help out.' She gestures around the room. 'And I don't see my dad anywhere. He's still in Thailand, isn't he? Can't even be bothered to come to his brother's wedding, let alone help out his own daughter.' Yo, she just finished him, and I think this would be a mic-drop moment, but Siobhan's eyes have started to fill with tears. Her uncle tries to say something again, but Siobhan shrugs him off and quickly walks away, shaking her head. This is kinda awkward because I missed my opportunity to storm off too, so now I'm just standing there in front of the bride and groom. OK, they're watching me. I don't know if I should say something or just leave. I do a tiny dance move where I shake my right leg in circles and I body pop my left arm like a chicken wing, it's proper entrée. They're staring at me with their mouths open. I think it's time to go find Siobhan.

Wedding Day: Part Three — The Climb Attic Finnarley

This place is like a maze, there's narrow corridors everywhere. Steam comes out into the hallway as I pass the kitchen. There's a big table with loads of hotplates, like the ones Aunt Tina brings to our large family gatherings. I can see chefs working and they're giving plates of food to the waiters, who are rushing in and out like sweaty ants. I pass a room that's empty except for two guys; I think one of them is practising his best-man speech. One day, I'll be doing that for Shanks when he marries Zendaya, just like we rehearsed.

I follow the corridor round to the fire exit at the end, but there's still no sign of Siobhan. I hear a knock, and my heart jumps because it might be her, but it's just one of the caterers who got locked out. I go to let him in; the fire exit only opens from the inside and he says, 'Thanks, mate, was just having a fag.' I don't want anyone else to get locked out, so I prop the door open with a chair and carry on my search for Siobhan. It's when I pass the disabled toilet that I hear crying inside. Oh my days, maybe Siobhan was here and she made someone upset. I decide to call out and ask if they've seen her.

'Hello? I'm sorry to interrupt your crying, but I'm looking for my friend.' The crying stops. 'She's got red hair and she's really beautiful, kinda like the Champions League theme tune or Prince Harry's mum.'

'Shaun, it's me.' I hear Siobhan's voice.

'Siobhan? What did you do to whoever's in there to make them cry?'

'No, Shaun, it's just me, I'm by myself.' I can hear her half laughing, half crying now. 'I was crying because I was upset.'

I don't get it . . . Other than today, Siobhan's usually bare composed and that. Well, except that time in Costa when I mentioned her mum. I wonder why she didn't come to the wedding. I don't mind, because I'm here instead and man's trying to be more reliable now.

Siobhan unlocks the door and says I can come in. Bruv. I'm not even allowed in a room with a girl with the door closed, let alone a toilet. Even though my mum's not at this wedding, her spies are everywhere. Yeah, recently we've been getting on, but I obey all the rules except gravity, diving in a swimming pool and doing the Mexican wave with more

186

than one person. I tell Siobhan that I can't be alone in a toilet with her because I'm claustrophobic. That's right, I'm scared of getting locked in a clauset. Also, if someone sees us and grasses me up, my mum is gonna ground me like minced beef. I say to Siobhan that I'll wait here until she feels less sad, and I won't ask her about her mum, and when she's ready we can go back to the table and eat a bit more food because I'm still hungry. If she doesn't want to, then that's OK too, I guess.

After a few minutes, she comes out. Her shoulders are quivering a little, and her eyes are still a bit bloodshot from crying, but we end up walking back to our table. She thanks me for waiting with her and links my arm as we cross the hall.

As we get back to our seats, we see that more food has been served while we were gone. No one looks up from their phones or asks where we disappeared to, I don't think they even realised we were gone.

The food in front of me is like a square block of meat. It smells kinda peng, and Siobhan tells me it's brisket. I don't know what animal it used to be when it was alive, but I'm too hungry to care. I'll just risk it for a brisket. I'm nearly finished before Siobhan has even had half of hers. She's barely eating, looking around the room, and I can tell she's still a bit upset about what her uncle said.

She looks at me and takes a deep breath. 'If I tell you what all this is about, promise you won't laugh at me or, even worse, feel sorry for me.' I want to reply, but my mouth is full of food. She carries on talking, but she's looking down at her lap. 'Me and my mum were in a car accident last year.' I swallow my food in a loud gulp. She doesn't look up. 'Mum went into a coma for two weeks and all I got was some broken ribs, a few bruises and a concussion. When I woke up in hospital and Mum wasn't there . . .' Siobhan pauses. She's holding back more tears. 'I thought she was dead. But she kept fighting, and eventually she woke up, only there was too much damage to her spine.' One tear escapes her eye, and then another and now there's loads of tears rolling down her cheeks. She quickly tries to wipe them off with a wedding napkin, but it don't matter because nobody notices. Everybody around us is on their phones and the rest of the party is too loud. 'My dad came to stay with me when Mum was in the hospital, but he'd already left my mum by then. He left again the minute he could. Mum's follow-ups from the hospital got less and less, and now it's my job to take care of her. I have to wash her and do the shopping and cook for us. I hate myself for thinking it, but I wish I had a normal life where none of this happened. I just want her to be my mum again.' She covers her face in her hands. 'We're on a waiting list to get the ground floor of our house converted to be more accessible. It's been ages though, and we don't know how much longer it'll be. The only other option is moving to a house that's already set up. Neither of us really wants to move though. Mum got a letter last week and the nearest place they can find for us is in Bristol.'

'Bristol? Is that even in London?'

'No, it's an entirely different city.' Siobhan sniffles. 'I'm sorry to spring all of this on you, you must think I'm such a monster. It sounds horrible, doesn't it? That we'd rather struggle here than move out there.' It kinda does, still. Things with my mum are much better these days, but I think back to all that time where we didn't really chat about stuff. I don't wanna think about Siobhan and her mum being forced to move away, I know how peak that feels. Siobhan opens her mouth like she's about to say something, then closes it and shakes her head like she changed her mind. Fam, all this time I been shook about having to leave, and now it looks like Siobhan is in the same boat, a bit like *Jaws* and *Titanic*. Even then, it sounds like Siobhan's sitch is way worse.

'Can't lie, I don't really understand, like, how mad does it get?'

'Of course you don't understand. Why on Earth would you?' Her voice is trembling when she talks. She's trying not to shout, but the others around the table don't care, some of them even have headphones on. 'Why would you ever need to understand what cooking three meals a day feels like? How could you understand what it's like to be constantly worrying about all the cooking, the cleaning, the shopping and laundry? Or what it's like to have to wash your mum from top to bottom every day? Who do you think puts on her socks, her underwear, her T-shirts? Who do you think cleans the house to stop it from becoming a pigsty? Who does the dishes every single bloody day? You think, because you only see me for one or two hours a week, that I'm not constantly exhausted, literally working my butt off a hundred and sixty-eight hours per week? I know Mum feels guilty sometimes, that I might be doing too much, even though I tell her I'm fine. I would do all the cleaning ten times over if it meant we didn't have to move to Bristol.' She starts mashing her food with a spoon, like really hard. I have to lean to the side to avoid friendly fire, and I'm glad the space next to her is empty.

Yo, can't lie, I'm kinda shook. In my head, Siobhan is picturing my face in that bowl.

She's crying again, so I do what Karen told me to do: I be a friend. I hug her, and she flings her arms around me, hugging me so tight I feel like I'm about to shatter into a million pieces. She's crying into my shoulder, and I know there's gonna be a wet patch on my blazer, but I don't mind. She keeps whispering, 'I'm sorry, I'm sorry.' I would say that I forgive her, but I don't think I'm the one she's apologising to. I know that she loves her mum, but obviously Siobhan is under a bit of stress. Maybe it's not my face in that bowl after all.

I need to never let go of her. Even when her quiet sobbing

stops and her breathing slows down to normal Homo-sapien levels, I know that on the inside I'll be hugging her forever.

'There's been a tonne of physiotherapy,' Siobhan says after a while. 'She's got full control of her right arm, and she can sort of wriggle her fingers on her left hand now, but they don't think she'll walk again.' She blows her nose on the napkin. 'The car that hit us came out of nowhere. Shaun, it came out of nowhere. I remember the brakes squealing and the look on my mum's face when it smashed into us. The last thing I remember before I passed out was his car door opening and two empty wine bottles falling out. Can you imagine – all of this because some drunken idiot ran a red light? It's not fair.' She's still sniffling a little.

Bruv, when I deep it everything makes sense now. This is why Siobhan has to rush home and cook, why she's homeschooled. It explains why everyone at this wedding feels sorry for her and keeps asking about her mum, why she was on one when she saw the wine on the table. For the first time I'm seeing Siobhan like a tree, so perfect to look at, such a perfect friend, but her bark and her branches are just as rough as mine. Jeez, remember when I knocked for her and she was all wet and out of breath and couldn't come out.

'Yo, Siobhan, that day you couldn't come out because you were all wet, I actually thought you were chasing a pigeon in your house.'

· 'A pigeon?' Siobhan smiles a bit. 'I would have trained it to send messages backwards and forwards from your house.'

'Yeah, that would have confused me, still. I wouldn't have much to say to a pigeon.'

'The messages would be to me, silly.' She stops smiling.

'It is kinda wild that you man aren't getting loads of help and that. Isn't there people out there who can step in?'

'It looked like we were going to get some carers assigned, then when no one showed up we were given some jargon about "cutbacks" and how they've had to "reprioritise staff".'

You know what – all these 'cutbacks' are actually starting to annoy me.

'I don't care,' Siobhan says. 'We've been managing this long on our own. And besides, they'd just be in our space every day and I don't need that. Our only real shot is getting the house adapted properly for Mum. The day you came over she'd had a bit of a fall.' She does a little groan of frustration. 'It's all been so messy, this business with waiting lists and being offered somewhere, but in Bristol. The worst part is not knowing. I'm hoping and praying my mum agrees to let us stay here.'

Me too, I can't lie. That feeling of not knowing where you're gonna live is rough, your insides feel like you're falling and they never hit the bottom. I don't want her to be going through that too.

Siobhan's eyes go distant, but she shakes her head again

192

to snap out of it. 'Hey, thank you. For listening to me, and not thinking I'm the worst human being on the planet.'

'I don't mind. I'm always gonna be your friend, regardless.' She's my tree.

She nudges my leg with her knee, and I don't know how it happened but we're actually holding hands. It's under the table but I don't care, it still counts. Bruh, I am so gassed. I have a huge smile on my face. She tries to keep a straight face, but her frown gives up and now she's smiling too.

Everyone's gotten up to watch the couple do their first dance to some moist Ed Sheeran song. Me and Siobhan stay sitting down, just talking and holding hands in secret. She tells me about how she hates being homeschooled and she tried to get out of it once by hiding under the bed. I tell her about the time me and Shanks bunked off school to go fishing in Burgess Park using wine gums on the end of a shoelace. I don't know how, but we both fell in and our clothes stank out the bus on the way home. The only thing I caught that day was a cold.

Eventually the wedding DJ puts on a song that Siobhan likes, some country singer who drives a van morrison. Siobhan grabs me by the hand and pulls me to the dance floor. I'm bare excited, and I try to move my arms, but I don't know how to dance to this music. I usually do freestyle breakdancing or the Cha Cha Slide but they won't work here.

'Just loosen up,' Siobhan says, throwing her arms in the

air. I think I'm getting it, my feet go left to right, and I just copy her, shaking our shoulders and singing badly along to the lyrics. When the song ends, we laugh and collapse onto each other and high-five. Another song starts. Oh no, it's Adele, and the music is slow and romantic. I don't know the words, but all around us people are pairing up.

I raise an eyebrow at Siobhan, and she does the same to me. It doesn't look like either of us is going back to the table to sit down. I bite my lip, this is a proper dalailama. She can sense that I'm nervous so she takes my hand and puts it on her waist. I'm touching a girl's waist. The song begins properly and we start swaying to the music.

As we dance, my hands are very careful not to move from the exact location she put them in. I'm so nervous I can tell I've started to sweat. Now I'm glad I'm wearing Adrian's old blazer, so Siobhan can't see the wet patches that are probably on my shirt.

'Shaun, can I ask you a question?' Her voice is so quiet I almost have to lean in to hear.

'Yeah, you can ask me anything, as long as it's not about crypto because I don't understand that stuff.'

'It's got nothing to do with crypto,' She shakes her head. 'I was actually going to ask, well, erm, do you think I'm pretty? It's just that right now, I feel I look a mess. You must think I look silly.' She says the last part really fast and looks away.

Do I find her pretty? She's got blotches of dried make-up

under her eyes, which are still a bit red from when she was crying earlier. And some strands of hair have come undone at the front and fallen down either side of her face.

'You are the prettiest person in the whole world,' I tell her. Yeah, my heart is beating a million miles per minute but, at the same time, this is so much easier than it was when I was trying to talk to Tanisha. 'You're so pretty that it makes me happy to think about your face because I live in the same world as something so stunning, it's like every second I see you could be a profile pic on Instagram. And the way your mouth moves when you talk, it makes me want to listen because your lips do this thing where they start smiling halfway through your sentence.' Now I'm really sweating because I've never said anything like that to anyone, ever. She doesn't reply, she just hugs me, properly wrapping her arms around me, while her head rests on my shoulder. She's got her eyes closed as I hug her back.

We carry on swaying, eyes closed, in the hugging position, long after Adele's song finishes. Even while the bride has a super meltdown behind us because one of the caterers tripped on a bottle of wine and poured an entire tray of glasses over her wedding gown. She's screaming, 'Who would leave a bottle of wine in the middle of the floor?'

And then the fire alarm goes off because someone jammed the fire exit open with a chair, and yet we still keep dancing. It's only after the panic settles, once everyone's got their belongings and the angry bride's shouting has started to die down, that me and Siobhan break out of our hug to go and grab some KFC.

We sat for ages in KFC, eating popcorn chicken and talking about everything, starting with our childhoods and ending with what we're gonna be when we grow up. Then we listened to some of the Wu-Tang album that Mr Rix recommended. Siobhan had the left headphone and I had the right one. It was live, we just chilled in our wedding outfits, listening to music until the staff started cleaning around us and Siobhan had to go. Her next-door neighbours were checking in on her mum, but Siobhan didn't wanna take advantage. She's so cool and considerate #rixword that means you care about other people more than yourself. She thanked me for being there for her today, and I know that I can do it all the time now.

I'm just getting home now, and the first thing I do is run to my room and message Shanks. Siobhan invited me to hers next time so I can meet her mum, which probably means I might actually go inside the house. I hope they don't ask me to take my shoes off like at Shanks' house; I once forgot to wear both socks, and my one foot smell was so extreme that I probably brought their neighbour's cat back to life. Going to her yard might be a big deal to Siobhan, but I didn't wanna hype it up too much in case it puts her off. Besides, I'm just gassed to spend more time with her.

Shanks is doing much better, but technically he's not supposed to be on his phone this late. I drop call him anyway, and he calls me straight back. I ask him about his news, but he doesn't have anything to report, so I dive straight into telling him about the wedding and the dance with Siobhan and the KFC. By the time I finish, I'm almost out of breath and we're both so excited that I slow-danced with a real girl and not a mop with a smiley balloon face sellotaped to it. After we hang up, I just flop onto my bed with a big grin on my face.

I'm kinda thirsty though, so I tiptoe to the kitchen, but the light's already on. Mum's sitting there at the table with her head in her hands, she looks up and forces a huge smile when she sees me walk in. My heart sinks a little bit when I see the letters around her with that big red writing at the top, but I'm still a bit too gassed to let it affect me.

'How was the wedding?' she asks.

'Honestly, it was kinda boring,' I tell her.

'Really?' She looks a little confused. 'Well, I'm sorry you had a bad day.'

'Oh, no, it's OK, because it was actually one of the best days ever.' I still can't stop smiling. 'I love you, Mum.'

She grins and nods, as if a part of her knows why I'm so happy. 'I love you too, son.'

The Spirit of Shakah-Khan

I love waking up in the mornings during the summer holidays, it feels different somehow. Like how air conditioning feels different to actually being outside, or how wearing clean socks is nicer than wearing the ones you find under the bed.

Before I even get out of bed, I can hear the tapping of the wooden spoon while Mum cooks, and I can hear Adrian watching his anime shows in the living room. I join him, and we both sit in silence, taking it in turns to skip the intro scenes at the beginning of each episode. It's a rare moment of truce, like when the English soldiers and the German soldiers played a five-a-side tournament on Christmas Day. I know about that because Mr Rix made a joke that the referee must have been from Switzerland because they were neutralised.

After breakfast Adrian starts a new episode, so I sneak out the living room to take a shower. Going first means I don't have to worry about the hot water running out. I like using Mum's shampoo because it smells exotic like Wonder Woman, gang-gang, and today it's super important that I smell at my best. You see, I'm meeting Siobhan's mum later and I need to make a good impression. I used to think that making a good impression is when you copy someone really well, but it's actually about tricking people into liking you before they realise how annoying you are.

I spoke on the phone to Shanks, and he said that it's a good idea for me to bring a gift, like a snack for grown-ups. I've seen on TV that adults usually bring wine or cheese to a dinner party, but I'm way too young to buy wine (and Siobhan hates it), so I stop by the shops on my way there and buy a packet of cheese, the square yellow ones that they put in burgers, because that's everyone's favourite type.

I could walk to Siobhan's house wearing a blindfold. I wouldn't, you know, because I'd probably bump into stuff and fall down a wishing well, but I could if I had to. You go past the bus stop, past the tree, and it's next door to the front garden that looks really nice. I'm listening to *The Chronic* by Dr. Dre on my way there. It's not as good as some of the others on the Rix list, this guy is so angry, but Snoop Dogg is on it and he tells some wild stories from his ends. I'm so hyped for Raptology, it's gonna bang.

When I knock for Siobhan, she isn't super excited like she usually is. She tells me we don't have to go in if I don't want to, but I tell her that it's calm and that I bought a gift. She looks at the packet of cheese that I'm holding up, and then she looks at me. She nods like she was expecting it, and tells me to come inside.

Yo, this is wild, I'm in Siobhan's house. I've been outside so many times, but to actually cross the front door must be how King Charles feels when he shops in-store at Argos. He'd probably buy loads of batteries or a cushion with a heart on it for his sidechick Camilla. We walk down the corridor and I look at some of the pictures hanging up, all of them are of Siobhan and her mum, but I can see a couple of nails where there used to be a photo and it's been taken down.

When we get to the kitchen at the end of the corridor, I'm surprised by how much space there is. The floors are wooden, there's a big table and sliding doors that lead out into a back garden that's a little messy. Siobhan's mum is in a wheelchair, and she's painting this giant picture of Peckham Square. It's so realistic I feel like I'm looking at Peckham Library through a window. Looking around, there's paintings everywhere. And not rubbish paintings like at school, I'm talking gallery quality, with the wooden frames and everything. Holy minestrone, did she paint all of these? Now I get why Siobhan was so gassed about going to the art gallery.

'Hi, Mum,' Siobhan says, putting my packet of yellow cheese slices straight in the fridge.

'Hello, petal,' her mum says. 'And this must be the young gentleman you're always talking about?'

Yo, Siobhan talks about me to her mum? I don't know why that makes my face all warm and smiley, but it does. Siobhan's blushing too. I'm gassed that her mum called me a young gentleman as well. It makes me feel like James Bond or one of those posh guys who knows how to use chopsticks. 'I'm Siobhan's mum, but you can call me Yvonne,' she says.

'Nice to meet you. I'm Shaun but you can call me Growls.' I remember what Shanks said earlier on the phone, he told me to say something nice about the house, so I give it a go. 'You have a very wonderful home, it reminds me of a house that's been spiritually cleansed.'

'Oh really? That's very nice of you to say.' She looks at Siobhan, who kinda smiles and shrugs. 'So have you been in many houses with spirits in them?' Yvonne looks interested, but Siobhan coughs loudly behind us.

'Yeah, my cousin who lived in Clerkenwell was being haunted by the spirit of Shakah-Khan. There was loads of moaning noises and clinking in the walls every time they used the taps. In the end, a plumber fixed the pipes that the ghosts lived in, and the evil stopped after that fateful day.'

'Right. Well, you'll be glad to know there's no spirits here.' This woman's bare safe. I don't know why Siobhan's standing in the doorway instead of joining us. Yvonne catches me staring at this cool painting hanging over the table. 'You like that one?' she asks with a little smile. 'It's been hanging in that same spot for thirteen years. Never moved.' Her smile disappears and she glances over at Siobhan. The painting is of a super cute baby with these puffy red cheeks and a little patch of ginger hair.

'Oh my days,' I say loudly. 'Is that Siobhan as a baby? No way, look at how cute you are. How old were you here, like five years old?'

'Seven months,' Siobhan corrects me. 'Hey, Mum, me and Shaun are going to go upstairs and watch TV.'

'OK, petal,' her mum says. But I'm not done looking at the painting. I go to stand in front of it. When you look at it closely, it's made of millions of tiny brush strokes, like little lines of colour that make a whole image when you step back.

'This is mad, the way you have all these little bits of colour, like tiny, but all together you get this sick painting.'

Yvonne looks shocked for a sec.

'That means it's good, Mum.' Siobhan jumps in.

'Oh, well, thank you very much, Growls, that's very sweet of you to say. Obviously, it's become a little more challenging than it once was.' She says it so casually, but I think she's

202

talking about the accident that made her disabled. I look to Siobhan for confirmation and Siobhan gives me a silent nod. Yvonne comes round to look at the painting with me. 'You see, the trick to adding tone is knowing where in the painting the light is coming from. If the light is here –' she points to the top corner – 'then the darker tones would be on the opposite side. Without the shadows, you wouldn't be able to tell where the light is coming from. And without either of those, well, there wouldn't really be any beauty at all.'

'Come on, Mum, he doesn't need to learn about this stuff.' Siobhan is tapping her foot, bare impatient. She's so pretty when she's impatient, but I'm honestly enjoying chatting to Yvonne.

'Was Siobhan this cute in real life?' I ask her.

'Cuter,' Yvonne says, smiling at her daughter. But Siobhan doesn't smile back. 'You kids, you grow up so fast, you know. One minute you're running around the house with your undies on your head, the next minute you're . . . you know.' She sighs. 'When I was pregnant, I had my heart so set on having a girl that we didn't even think about boys' names. This little baby is all I ever wanted.'

'Yo, that's a lot. And after all of that, you had a daughter. What are the chances?'

'Oh, I'd say about fifty-fifty,' Siobhan chimes in. 'Mum, can we go upstairs now?' Yvonne lets us go, and I see her move back over to continue painting as we leave the room.

I follow Siobhan upstairs and I'm noticing more photos hanging up and more spaces where photos used to be. There's also bare paintings, but some are dark, some are light and some are places in London that I've been before but can't remember the names. Siobhan's room is super tidy, but I notice bare clothes have been kicked under the bed, just like what I do when Mum tells me to clean my room. Does this mean girls are messy like boys are? The pillows on her bed are purple with flowers, but the bedsheets are the ones from Marvel's *Infinity War* and it gives me this wonderful upwards feeling in my stomach. There's posters everywhere, and some cool drawings that she's done of different manga characters fighting each other. Yo, this is my dream room.

'I'm sorry about my mum,' Siobhan says. 'I know she can go on and on, but you don't have to be polite, you can just tell her if she's talking too much.' I know she's talking to me but I'm too distracted, we're sitting on the bed and the pillows smell bare peng. 'That's lavender spray. Shaun, can you focus?'

'What? Yeah, nah, your mum's cool. And her art is kinda amazing. Yours too,' I tell her, looking around the room. On a level, though, I kinda like Yvonne. She doesn't look at me the way people at the wedding were looking at me. Sometimes, people see me and the energy in the room changes like a dehumidifier. I think it happened a little bit in the National Gallery too. Siobhan is biting her nails, so I can tell something's up. And I can't help thinking it's because of me being here. 'Hey, you OK? You been acting a bit weird today.' She doesn't immediately respond, so we just sit there in silence. I think I know what this is about.

'You do?'

'Yeah, I think so. Are you embarrassed of me? Is that why you don't like me talking to your mum?' I have to ask because it's the only thing that makes sense. Siobhan's eyes are wide open in shock.

'Of course not. God, no, Shaun, I'm not embarrassed of you, not at all.' She looks bare horrified that I'm upset.

'Well, what is it then?'

'It's nothing.' She covers her face with her hands. 'Well, it's the exact opposite of what you're thinking. I'm the one who's actually embarrassed. Look, I guess I'm just not used to people seeing this part of my life. Sorry if I've been a bit awkward.' I tell Siobhan that she hasn't been awkward. Awkward is when your mum walks into your room and finds you going to town on your own bellybutton with a sharp pencil, or when your IT teacher catches you asking Google if you can get eye infections from farting in the bath. There's levels to this.

'Oh my God, did those things actually happen?'

'Don't watch that.'

'Well, either way, you do know how to make me feel better.' She pokes her tongue out. I like that she doesn't mock it, she's not like most people. Once in a sweet shop someone heard me call the guy behind the counter my sugar daddy. He wasn't even leng. Everyone at school was savage after that.

For real, that's the thing about chilling with Shanks and Siobhan, I know that I can be myself around people and I don't need to front anything. But I still can't help thinking about the other MCs at Raptology, like, what if they clock that I ain't one of them? I like growing up on road, but I'm not hood like Adrian, he's always going on about how weak I am. Sometimes I think I'm too ratchet for fancy weddings, but not tough enough that they take me seriously in my ends. Life's peak when you don't fit in anywhere, and Raptology can make or break me. If I flop at this competition, what will I have left?

'You've got me. And you've got Shanks, and you'll still have your family.' I guess so. 'Growls,' she says, using my maiden stage name, 'whether you're killing it in your rap competition, or riding your bike, or up a mountain in the Himalayas, you're still you, and you're an artist. The same as those painters you admired in the gallery. You got this, you're going to smash it, because you're amazing and talented.' She's so intense, and she got me bare hyped up. She thinks I'm amazing and talented and proper hench, these MCs won't know what hit them.

'Thanks. Like, for real, that really means a lot to me.' We're both smiling and Siobhan's blushing, we don't really know what to say to each other.

'Shall we put this film on?' Right, yeah, I forgot about that. We put it on, and it's about this little girl who gets spirited away to some next universe where nothing makes sense. I forget what the film's called, but it's super boring. One star. Siobhan called it timeless, and I agree because it just goes on and on. How is it an anime but there's no powers or swords or cool dudes with spiky hair? This is more boring than when I played a rock in the school nativity, all curled into a ball and that. But Siobhan likes it, and we are sitting very close to each other. Even with this dead film on, there's nowhere else I'd rather be.

Siobhan fell asleep on me. We were watching the film, and after a while she just rested her head on my shoulders. I found the TV remote under the pillow I was sitting on and managed to reach it without waking her up. Now I'm on episode 3 of *Falcon and the Winter Soldier* or *Handmaid's Tail* or whatever this is. Can't lie, I could stay here all day and all night, with the TV on and the weight of Siobhan's head on my arm.

It's almost 7 p.m. when I get a text message from Adrian, telling me to come home quick. It's odd because Adrian never texts me, not even on my birthday to tell me he loves me or anything. When I don't answer straight away he starts calling, and the vibration makes me jump. Annoyingly, it also wakes up Siobhan, who asks if everything's alright. I tell her that it's fine, but I'm gonna have to bounce. The phone goes off again, another text from Adrian saying, 'Where r u?' and I have to drag myself away from Siobhan. She looks tired and a bit confused, and I want to stay with her forever, but something is definitely up with ,my brother.

I go to say goodbye to Yvonne on the way out. She's on the phone and it's playing classical from the loudspeaker.

'Hello, love. Sorry, I spend most of my time on hold to these people, housing associations are a nightmare. All of this is such a palava.' She's so talented, making pavlova and phone calls like it's nothing. I don't really wanna go, but I hope I'll be back soon.

'It was wonderful having you.' She's so nice. I guess she must have found the packet of cheese that I bought, Shanks was right. The entire way home, I'm thinking about Siobhan. Even though I'm outside, an inside part of me is still up there in her room.

26

Home Is Where Your Stuff Is

Before I've even gotten out the lift, I can tell something's wrong. I can hear Mum shouting, and she's not holding back. Some people across the balcony are filming, and Daphne who lives a few doors down is outside in her dressing gown. As I'm running out, my stomach turns to ice when I see what's going on. Of course. Gregory Flynn is back, but this time he's got backup, some hench bald guy in a black T-shirt and a little woman holding a clipboard. Mum is fully screaming at the visitors, and Adrian's holding her back from trying to swing at them. The T-shirt guy is standing in front of Gregory Flynn like a bouncer, arms folded and smiling.

They barely flinch when they see me running towards them, but the little woman with the clipboard is trying to calm everything down.

'Ms Thompson, please, it doesn't have to be like this. We're giving you until the end of the month to get your things together, we're trying to be reasonable.'

'Reasonable? Reasonable? And what about my boys? You think it's reasonable for them to be on the street?' Mum's stopped struggling, but Adrian is still holding her back.

Gregory Flynn finally pipes up. 'Well unfortunately, you've been avoiding my calls, and we've now had to come out of our way, just to make sure you'll comply when the time comes. I wasn't sure that you understand how pressing this is.' His voice is bare slow and patronising. 'You seem quite ungrateful, considering I've personally taken time out of my schedule to come over and communicate this to you.'

Mum kicks off again, and Adrian has to tighten his grip. The sides of Gregory Flynn's mouth are twitching like he's trying not to laugh. Mum's swearing at him, using language we'd never be allowed to say. The little woman touches Gregory Flynn on the shoulder, whispering something in his ear, and they both look at me. He looks a bit disappointed, but he nods and they turn to leave.

'We'll be back next Monday, the 1st of August, with a crew. If you haven't left by then, you'll be trespassing on the property and we'll be forced to call the authorities.'

We're all in the kitchen, Mum is sitting at the table crying while Adrian rubs her back. He's bare screwing me from across the kitchen.

'Where were you the whole time? Probably with your little girlfriend when your family needed you.' Why is he so vexed at me?

'I had no idea things were going to go down. How was I supposed to know?'

'Don't give me that, I was calling you for ages. And when you did turn up, you were just standing there like the useless chicken that you are.'

'What was I supposed to do? Chase them away?' I can feel tears pricking my eyes.

'Whatever. On my life, this family can't rely on you for nothing. You're such a loser.' His words sting. Maybe he's right.

'Boys, that's enough.' Mum finally looks up. 'It's bad enough we've got these people on our case, we shouldn't be fighting among ourselves. Now, I need you both to think about what to pack.' Adrian looks like he's about to say something more, but Mum interrupts him. 'Both of you, I mean it.'

We start walking out, but Adrian kicks one of the chairs, sending it flying across the kitchen. He barges me with his shoulder as he passes, and I stumble into the door frame. Mum doesn't even say anything, she's got her back to us and she sounds like she's crying again.

After Adrian stormed out, Mum left the kitchen too. She

put her hand on my shoulder and she didn't say anything, so now I'm just in my room. All of this is a bit next. Maybe Adrian's right. But I didn't see him come up with any ideas. At least I'm doing Raptology. And what's his problem with Siobhan, why did he even mention her?

I try calling Siobhan but she's not picking up. She always picks up. Her landline is upstairs, and she's usually on it super quickly. Shanks isn't picking up either, but it's late, and I know he still has a curfew.

I start scrolling through my phone, something I haven't done in ages, not since I started properly hanging out with Siobhan. I guess it's a nice distraction, and a good way to get my screen time up again. But scrolling through IG, everything I used to find interesting is really boring.

Raptology is only a couple days away now, and if I mess it up then it looks like curtains. I'll be holding the biggest 'L' of a lifetime. This might well be my one shot, my one moment, to make everything right. To look in the mirror and be someone I can be proud of. Yo, am I ready for this?

Am I steady for this?

Man's pleading for another season of Growls doing plenty of bits,

I ain't having any of this,

I'm coming back blowing up like Guy Fawkes treason,

It's comeback season, crown me like aperitif,

They call me Comeback King for a reason.

*And if any of this rings a bell, you tell them I'm Annie coz
life is a hard knock hotel,*

But it's the only one I got, so go, go spell it out

Coz I vowel to be back like a new track from Adele.

*All knowing, got my lyrics prepped like private school but
I'm not going,*

Showing up coming up show'em up this is tough,

Call my bluff but you don't have bluff's number,

Open your ideas from slumber, jack, bring it back,

Spitting bars while they snicker like a Mars in a value pack.

Don't ever watch that, Growls is back, baby.

The *Toy Story* Theme Tune
But Only Opposite

I haven't heard from Siobhan since things kicked off on the balcony with those housing officers. Maybe she caught feelings because I dipped so quickly, but you know it really wasn't my fault. She ain't been picking up her phone or nothing. She knows the competition is tomorrow, and I have to make sure she's gonna be there. Like, I can't do it without her, especially if Shanks won't be there. I've been pacing by the door, trying to make my mind up on if I should go see her. You know what, I got nothing to lose.

I'm grabbing my hoodie. Racing out onto the balcony, I almost bump into Sharon. She asks if my mum is home and I shout, 'Yeah, probably,' over my shoulder as I pace it to the lift. As soon as I'm out on the street, literally when my shoes hit the pavement, I carry on sprinting all the way to her house #cardio #blessedwindcarryme. I knock on the door and wait for her to answer.

OK, it's been twenty seconds so I knock again, a bit louder this time. Fam, nobody's answering, I'm getting anxious. Even if Siobhan's out, surely her mum would have answered by now. This is getting long, so I sit on the doorstep and wait for them to come back. I'm biting Tic Tacs in half and feeding them to pigeons to pass the time. Waiting can be really boring, but it's not that deep. The neighbours are approaching their door, some old couple with shopping. While the guy's keys jingle, the lady looks over the fence at me.

'Can I help you, young man?' she asks.

'I'm just waiting for Siobhan? I don't think she's in so Imma just wait here for her.' I must look proper desperate. I haven't felt this pathetic since the time I went to the GP and a cockroach fell out my pocket. The old lady's face relaxes when she replies.

'Oh, you've just missed them. The van came for their stuff this morning.'

'Their stuff?' What is she talking about?

'Well, yes, they've moved to Bristol.' She starts tutting. 'These houses just aren't accessible, that poor girl was doing far too much. Always in and out with the shopping, bless her.'

Nah, surely Yvonne wouldn't do that, she called me a

fine young man. Why is this neighbour woman lying to me? Then again, I remember something that Siobhan said at the wedding, about how her mum feels guilty that she's been doing so much. And I'm pretty sure Yvonne was on the phone to some housing people when I left the other day. Is this real? Can they really be gone?

'Young man, you can sit on that doorstep till you're blue in the face. But I'm afraid you'll be waiting a long time. It's probably best for you to go home, dear.' That's ridiculous, only Smurfs are blue in the face. My face is getting hot as the tears rise up. I'm blue in the heart.

My head is spinning now as it all sinks in. The old lady makes one more tutting noise and goes inside. I take a step back and look up at the windows to see if maybe the curtain's moving or something else that tells me it isn't true. I can't move, my legs are rooted to the spot. What is going on? Bristol's not even Zone 6, let alone London.

She didn't even get to say goodbye. I turn to leave, but my legs feel like jelly, and every step away from her house makes me turn to look up at the window for one last hope. We're best friends, and best friends are there to hug each other and help each other feel better when the other one's sad. And now I've lost Siobhan, and my whole body feels like it's driving down a steep hill.

I'm still struggling to move, but I do manage to get out of her front garden and into the street. This is so unfair.

How is life so peak for no reason? How can I do Raptology without her or Shanks?

When I get in, I sink into my favourite chair in the kitchen. Adrian is grabbing a drink from the fridge and he stops when he sees me sitting there. He hovers like he's about to walk out, but then he sighs and asks me what's wrong. I open my mouth to tell him, but nothing comes out. He folds his arms, waiting for me to answer, and when he turns to leave I just start crying like some wasteman. Bare tears and my nose is leaking like a three-year-old's.

'Yo, why you crying like that? Did someone hurt you? Did they rob you? Oi, give me names, on my life, I swear I'll sort it out. Where are they?' He's so loud that it actually shocks me out of crying. I feel like an electrical charge in my chest. For once, he's not vexed at me, he's vexed *for* me.

'It's my friend, the girl that you saw me with. She's gone. And I miss her.'

'Oh.' Now he just looks uncomfortable, he's frowning at the door like he wants to run out and drink his sweet nectary juice. In the end he forces himself to pull up the other chair and asks me what happened. I don't even know where to begin, so I start telling him about how me and Siobhan met in the cage on a mad fluke, and she taught me that there's so many cool things out there I never knew about, like galleries and coffee shops and Italian food. I segway into telling him about Shanks, about how he got really ill and tired, and about my meetings with Karen. And then worst of all, that Gregory Flynn guy kicking us out of here. I'm so shook of being homeless, it's unreal. What's going to happen if we have to cut from ends? My friends need me, and I need them. Even now, Adrian's just sitting there, ice cold, like an ice-ice baby. Surely I'm not the only one with something to lose.

'Aren't you worried about *your* friends? You don't seem like you even care about us leaving. I been scared, and I've got this chest bubble that comes, and everything feels like it's crashing down. It seems like you don't feel any of that.' When I say it, Adrian's frown is so intense. He's like the KKK watching *Black Panther* in 3D at the IMAX.

'Fam, of course I'm scared. You think I ain't thinking about it all day, every day? I ain't tryna be cold, I'm tryna stay calm.' He looks up at the ceiling and bites his tongue. Wow, I wonder if he's been chatting with Karen too, it just feels kinda next that me and Adrian have been reacting the same way. He usually never talks about emotions, I've never seen him like this. 'I just, I get all this pressure that I need to do Dad's job, to protect you and Mum, but I know that I can't. I'm supposed to keep us safe, but I can't even stop getting stop us getting evicted.' Wow. So that's why he's been moving salty.

I used to think that Adrian was so gangsta I wanted to

be just like him. I never knew that all this time he's been trying to be a hero, but trying so hard that he's forgotten how to just be himself. I don't need him to be my dad, I just need him to be my big brother. He's been dealing with the eviction on the inside, which is different to me doing everything I can on the outside to get through it. I start telling him all about Raptology, about the prize money and how I've been training my English skills with Mr Rix. This is my chance to make things better. And he can't tell Mum because I don't want her to get her hopes up in case I don't win. Adrian agrees not to tell her, she's stressed enough as it is.

'By the way, I'm not gangsta,' he says. 'I did a dumb thing once, but that's not who I am no more.' I'm remembering the police knocking on our door, with Mum wilin' out, and all the hours we spent sitting around in Citizen's Advice. 'We look forward, not back, and I think no matter what you do tomorrow, we can be whoever we wanna be.' He's not looking me in the eye when he says that, it's almost like he's talking to himself. 'I didn't want you looking up to me when I was doing a madness. That's why I ain't really been about.' I ask him if he still does a madness sometimes, if that's how he always has money for takeaway. He smiles slyly. 'It's less of a madness. Just some online stuff. Don't watch that.' Adrian doesn't want me to be like him.

'But at least you're strong,' I tell him. 'You could probably fight anything and anyone and still win. I'm just a nobody, I can't even stop my friends from leaving and getting ill. There's no way I can win Raptology.'

'Shaun, you were never a nobody. Legit, I'm sorry if I made you feel that way. Maybe I'm too hard on you sometimes. I think it gets to me, you know, but I shouldn't take it out on you.' He's still not looking at me when he talks. 'You're some capable yoot. Believe me, you got a different kind of strength in you, me and Mum can both see it. What would that Siobhan girl say if she heard you talking like this? Or Shanks? Or Mr Rix or your counsellor?'

They would want me to do Raptology.

And you know what? I'm going to go to this competition in beast mode, and when I win, I'll do it for us all. And then I'll go celebrate with Siobhan, wherever she is. I don't care, I'd walk all the way to Bristol or China, or anywhere in the world, just to make her smile on a rainy day. I would walk for months. I would swim and run and crawl across all the rivers and roads, all of them, until I see her. And my heart would never get tired, not in a billion years.

This one's for her, for Shanks, for my fam, for the entire block! I don't need to be a thug, Imma always be a G on road.

'It sounds like you got this, bro.' Adrian says. 'You just got to believe in you, everyone else does. I know I do.'

'Swear down?'

'On my life.'

28

Spitting More Bars Than a Sheep in a Corner Shop

I couldn't sleep last night, I had all these thoughts in my head while I was lying there. Looking around my empty room, the bags that I packed in case we do get kicked out are just sitting in the corner like a beanbag chair that takes you two to three working days to get up out of. Even if I don't win Raptology, I need to be someone who tries. Even Adrian has my back so, win or lose, I'm going out like bang-bang sauce.

Sourcing my rhymes with a minute's deadline,
MCs recline when I eat them, no remorse,
Best believe I'll be back for seconds, thirds, fourths.

Whatever happens from here, homeless or not, I got the best friends and family in the world. Karen told me to be a hero, and a real hero goes down swinging.

The event is taking place in St Thomas' School, which is where Adrian did his GCSEs. He used to tell me that I can't even spell GCSE, let alone get one. I have to sneak out the house; if Mum found out what I was doing she'd probably flip and I don't need her asking questions in the fifth degree. I hold my shoes in my hand as I tiptoe out past the kitchen. Adrian silently opens the front door in a way that it doesn't creak, he's had loads of practice at that. He pats me on the shoulder and quietly says, 'Good luck, bro.'

It's weird to be going to a school in my own clothes. I feel like Batman sneaking into Coachella. Getting closer to the school, there's young road mans gathering in the street. And it's not just performers. I see families pulling up, people's friends, everyone's got their peeps. I reach out to grab my mum's hand, but I'm grabbing air because I'm here completely on my jacks.

I scope out the competition as I get to the entrance; there's little groups of freestyles happening in small batches as people get their last-minute practice in. They're good. They're really good. But I'm not terrible either. I hurry past them and go straight into the school.

I have to sign in at the check-in desk first. When the lady asks my name, I ask her if she wants my MC name or my real name.

She rolls her eyes. 'What name did you use to sign up?'

'My real name, Shaun.'

'OK, and what's your surname?'

'Sir Shaun.' I've never met the king, but I'm pretty sure that's what it would be.

It takes a while, but we find my name on the list eventually. Giving the lady my middle names, Bethany Ezekiel Frenkel, might have confused the situation. It's difficult to concentrate because I'm too amped up. When she asks me if I have a guardian with me, I just tell her my mum is in the loo because she had one of those tear gas kind of poos where she's leaving remnants of her soul in the toilet. The check-in lady hurries me along after that, she doesn't want to hear more details. I don't blame her, my made-up story is disgusting. All the adrenaline is getting to me. If Siobhan was here I would be making less mistakes. Or 'fewer mistakes', as she'd say.

I follow a family up the stairs to the second floor, where all the noise is coming from. When we get to the school hall, the scene is kinda wild. It looks like they've set it out for an assembly, except there's cameras pointed at the stage and people with badges running around, and we're all wearing our fleekest garms. Man's wearing my nicest blue top, inside-out to help hide the stain, and my favourite gold (painted) chain that I found on the bus. The front seats are for judges and organisers, but there's bare heads in the audience, and not just kids my age – lots of parents and friends have turned up too. There's a little burn in my heart when I think about the fact that I'm all alone like a Bounty at the bottom of a box of Celebrations.

The hall is filling up pretty quickly now. The clock tells me we're starting in seven minutes. MCs are being gathered on either side of the stage, and I finally see who I'm up against. Bruh, I can't do this. These kids look hard, I thought there was supposed to be an age limit on this ting? Why do they all look so much older than me? Everyone here looks like they would chew me up and spit me out, a bit like when I tried that olive.

I clock some people giggling when they see me, they probably think I'll be an easy target. And let's be honest, I ain't got Kendrick's flow or Dave's lyrics or Ty Dolla $ign's national currency. But what I do have is a peculiar set of skills.

They announce the competitors and explain the rules. There's eight of us, four on either side, and we'll battle head-to-head in pairs. The MCs that make it through each round will battle each other until only two MCs are left standing for the final.

As the first contestants battle it out, I'm zoning at the quality of these peeps, they ain't holding back. It's just bar after bar, tearing each other apart, flowing beats like the River of Babylon.

At the end of each battle, the announcer asks the audience to make some noise. They cheer really loudly, but the judges make the final decision. Look at them, 'consulting' with each other like a witches' coven. My heart drops when the judges finally name the winner of the battle and I suddenly notice there's no one in the line ahead of me. I'm next. The guy opposite is wearing a do-rag and he's bare screwing me, no doubt choosing the lyrics he's gonna finish me with.

The announcer calls us up to the stage, now there's definitely no chance I can run away.

29

Growls vs Young Mystik

'Please put your hands together for our next MC from Camberwell, Abass Kendeh, AKA Young Mystik.' The audience goes wild, and his family over in one corner are bare hyped, stomping their feet and clapping their hands like he just saved the *Titanic* from that giant lettuce. The announcer looks at her sheet of paper. 'And next to join us onstage is someone who's new to the scene, please give a warm welcome to Shaun Thompson, AKA Bethany Frenkel, from Peckham.' Yo, why this woman using my middle name for? The audience are polite, but my round of applause is much quieter than Mystik's.

I grab the mic, look at the audience and gulp. 'My name's Growls, not Bethany. But hey, names are there to be broken.'

The audience is silent. A hundred blank faces stare up at me. Somebody coughs.

The organiser takes the microphone back. Mystic laughs at me and flashes his bare grills that look like he's been eating tinfoil for breakfast. He bops onstage, all confident like a doctor at a pharmacist convention, taking the mic back from the host. 'Without further ado, DJ spin that track.'

'Yo, look at this guy, Growls, you're a mess.
Did nobody tell you, you're dealing with the best,
Challenging me was a mistake, you'll be put to the test,
And you'll join the other losers as the worst of the rest.
Coming at you like a disease, I go as I please,
Blistering lyrics that will make you freeze.
I'm rolling with Gs, I'm stacking up Ps,
I'm the rap god while you pray on your knees.
I'm driving a whip and I'm taking your keys,
I'm burning hot and I got you turning around,
Walk on, it's a hundred degrees.
I ain't never running out of bars, I got lyrics galore,
Your rhymes are like your bank account, they're both staying poor.
I'm winning this battle, leave the crowd wanting more,
And you just got hammered, like Thanos and Thor.'

Damn, that was sick. Well, except the part where he claims to drive, we both know he's too young. This guy just ended me though, and I might as well leave now. What was I thinking, coming here?

Two of the judges look impressed, and the audience are all applauding. Looking out at them, they seem to be loving it. I can see on their faces, none of them is mocking it, they seem to be vibing to his bars. That guy's clapping. That person's whooping. But then someone catches my eye, staring straight up at me, it can't be . . .

Mr Rix.

And next to him, still looking weak, but it's definitely him, it's Shanks! And Adrian is there too, and he's brought Mum with him. And they've all found each other. If dreams had dreams, this is what they would be. Yo, this is too much madness, I wanna cry and jump off the stage and run towards them.

I'm not alone. Looking at these man in the crowd, I was never alone.

Shanks looks kinda skinny, like he's still worn out, and his hairline is in desperate need of a shape-up, but it's still my boy and I'm here onstage for him, for our friendship, for honour. Adrian is holding his phone up like he's filming and Mum just looks amused. Mr Rix still looks like a teacher, wearing a suit and tie like he's going to court for eating a swan. He's nodding, like he knows I can do this. I remember what he told me, about how my opponents are gonna hype themselves up and talk about fake gangster stuff. I'm

better than that. I'm different. I can tell a story. I got this.
The music starts.

'OK, you lied when you said you're the best,
I'm not the best either, but the crowd are impressed,
Impressed by your breath, now the back row know 'bout
the faint smell of death.
Your bars are as useful as a door hinge in foreign storage,
Stupid egg with no cress, puff your chest and I still couldn't
care less.
If the audience wanna know about me, I'll tell you straight
off the bat,
In fact, I am no G, I locked myself in a pram, that's how
moist I can be,
And I ran when that mum saw me sitting still in the seat.
She gave me beats like Dre and I was off like a rocket,
For security, I zip my keys in my pocket,
But I might get evicted. Not a thing that can stop it,
Except if the crowd shouts louder for the bars that I'm
dropping,
Carry on your fake hood life but I'm a neek and ain't
stopping.
Like a Pringle at a party, I'm just keeping it popping.

The audience are silent for a few seconds, and then they
erupt with applause. People are whooping and lots of them
are laughing, but in a good way for once. Everyone's on
their feet, and even the judges are smiling and nodding. My

229

section of the crowd are cheering and whooping, and it feels like there's a balloon of golden joy that's inflating inside of me. I'm still a little nervous when I see the organiser asking the judges for their verdict. She nods and smiles as she joins us onstage. My fingers are crossed behind my back.

'The winner, by unanimous decision, is . . . Shaun Thompson, AKA Growls, AKA Bethany.'

I can't believe it, I'm through. I'm on top of the world, like the North Pole, or Australia in the winter.

The audience clap us offstage, but I see Mystik getting angry, he's tryna have a go at the judges. He doesn't climb off the stage straight away, he only leaves when the crowd start murmuring.

As soon as I'm down, I run into the crowd to find everyone. Mr Rix goes to shake my hand, but I jump right in for the hug with Shanks. Adrian and my mum join in the hug too, while Mr Rix stands there nodding and smiling. Swear down, I feel like the Grinch when his heart grew and grew, I know that I got everything I need right here.

Me and Shanks are chatting back and forth and making a bit of a scene.

'I can't believe you're here, bruv, it's really you!' I poke his face to make sure he's not a hollow gram.

'I was never gonna miss it. MC Squared for life, even if I ain't up there with you.'

Some of the other MCs are looking over screw-faced,

but I don't care. It's only when the last battle of the first round begins that I start to pay attention. The girl on the mic is killing it. The way she spits is pure fire, like a shiny Charizard vs a level 3 Pidgey. The guy she's battling looks like he's about to cry. The crowd are making bare noise, going 'ohhhh' every time she drops a bar.

Mr Rix can tell what I'm thinking, man's got a fifth sense, and he puts his hand on my shoulder. 'You've got this, Shaun, and whatever happens, we're all proud of you.' Mr Rix is so calm, it's the opposite of how I feel. Shanks nods in agreement and tells me I'm gonna kill it. Adrian keeps telling me he's getting it all on camera, and Mum is cleaning my cheek with her thumb that she licked.

'I can't believe you boys. I thought Adrian was pulling my leg when he told me what you were doing.' She's proper embarrassing, her thumb's seriously rubbing up my face. Glancing over at Adrian, he just shrugs, looking sheepish.

OK, I'm officially gassed. Even though my cheek has been rubbed sore, it means everything that they're here, they got my back. Swear down, I got this.

30

Growls vs Thuggy B

The lady's calling the remaining contestants back to the stage and I have to go take my place. The guy in front of me has to battle the mean girl, I don't envy him. I try to wish him good luck, but he airs me, man doesn't even turn around. If that was me, I would turn round like a broken compass and run out of here. She gon' eat him for breakfast, lunch and dinner, on some healthy eating habits wave. I just stare at the back of his fresh trim until he's called up.

The crowd is more hyped than they were in the first round, they proper make bare noise every time a hot bar is dropped. My guy who ignored me is pretty good, but the girl is better. She's called MC Moneypenny and I quickly Google her to see what I'm up against. I think of Siobhan when I use Google because I know she don't have it; my heart kinda hurts that she's not here.

Moneypenny has over 800 views on her last YouTube post. It's not even anything mad, just her freestyling in a park. I'm thinking about my underwear video and how many views that had, probably more than Moneypenny, but that ain't a good thing.

Before I know it, the battle is over. She just brushed him aside like a girl's weave blowing down the street like a tumbleweed. You know them ones, when it's evening, and the salon is still open, and there's some little, happy kids running in and out, it's like that.

Finally they call me and my competitor up. I lose the toss, so I'll be going first this time. Thuggy B looks like a true thug out here. He's bigger than me, and stronger than me, but I have strength too. I can throw an entire orange over one metre away, ain't no holdup. Dress me like a ballerina because it takes tutu tango. He turns to look at me with a big grin on his face. He silently holds up his phone, flashes the screen at me, and my stomach plummets into ice water. He has the poo-pants video. He's playing it on mute as he walks onstage.

I'm finished. It's curtains for me now. If he plays that video, I'm gonna get laughed out by the entire room, not just the other rappers. I look into the crowd and see Shanks clapping, going wild. Mr Rix, next to him, gives the nod of approval. I can't leave. I breathe in, and out. There's only one thing I can do to win this. I need to tell my own story. Man, I hope this works. I take the mic.

'Yo, everyone, it's me again, Growls,
Need to clear a couple things up, no paper towels,
But I got another story to tell – if you'll allow,
Been smiling somehow, behind the tears of a clown.
So don't get it twisted,
I went viral, just in case you missed it,
Floating up in a balloon, ah yeah I stay long-winded,
Dirty laundry out online and now I'm staying listed,
But all the hate that came my way will be the strength you witness.
Yo, Thuggayyyy, my story got this crowd invested,
And your lyrics are basic, face it,
This is just my greatness tasted.
Nah, I'm just playing. I'll even sign pants for ya,
Might go up cliffs in Dover, breathing deep like in yoga.
Yeah my doo-doo got views but you still medicocre, you the weediest ogre,
End your credits like I'm Marvel.
Cutscene. Your movie's over.
And I'm majestic. See this crowd wanna see me tested
But that's not me v. Thuggy B,
The last rapper I bested.'

Yo, the audience is loving it. One of the judges is laughing so hard it looks like he's crying. Thuggy B is the only person in here who doesn't crack a smile, man's like Nick Fury judging a baking contest.

He waits for the noise to die down and then he takes the mic for himself.

'Yo, this isn't just bants, this guy right here literally did a poo in his pants.

He's a loser, I'm a cruiser, this crowd won't choose ya,

When they find out what happened in your pants, they'll sue ya.

Hey everyone, look at my phone,

Look what this guy does when he thinks he's home alone.

His mum comes in to clean and she holds up his poo,

What can you do, this guy has no clue!

He should leave now coz we all know the truth,

He's not worthy for the stage,

If he doesn't leave now he might doo-doo on you.

You see this video, does it ring any bells?

You just got finished, plus your underwear smells.

That was aite, still, but the audience aren't reacting to him anything like the same way they did with me. Mum and Adrian are screwing him, I don't think they liked the way he was sending them kinda shots. All he had was underwear jokes. I think the judges kinda sense it too, because they're looking around to see the people's reaction. It doesn't take them very long to announce that I'm through. The crowd starts clapping and I clap them back. Damn, I'm the best at being humble. Someone whistles and I'm getting gassed, I'm grinning from rear to rear.

I don't have to leave the stage because we're doing the final battle now. The energy is different, it feels electric. All the rappers who lost and everyone they're with are in the room making noise. The place is bouncing, people are cheering and chatting. I'm just waiting for MC Moneypenny to come up. The way she's been moving these last few rounds, I got more chance of winning a dance battle with two left feet where my eyes should be. The butterflies in my stomach are so big they must've been hungry-hungry caterpillars in a past life, a mystifying existence. My hand is trembling, I'm starting to sweat.

And then I see it. A flash of red hair, and my favourite face in the whole world. My stomach drops like a mixtape. She's trying to peer over the crowd, out of breath and sweating like she ran here. I can't believe it. Siobhan's here. And suddenly all the fear of facing Moneypenny is gone. It's like someone's just turned on the lights when I didn't even know it was dark. I'm bulletproof, like a stab proof vest, and suddenly nothing matters any more, because my friends are here, my family is here, the Avengers have truly assembled. Who the hell is Moneypenny? What is Raptology? For the first time I feel like a real rapper, and it's got nothing to do with popping bottles by the pool. I deserve to be here.

Even Moneypenny looks a bit nervous as she scans the crowd. When she bops onstage, though, her rap persona is back and she's trying to look even meaner than before. Her grills look like knife teeth, it's like she wants to bite my head off like when you eat a jelly baby. The round hasn't even started yet, but she grabs the mic off the announcer.

'I don't even know what you're doing here, you're a nobody,' she says to me. 'Why don't you go back into the crowd and hug your boyfriend some more?'

Yo, that's kinda homophobic, still, and why she coming after Shanks like that? Now she's got me angry for Shanks *and* the LBLT community. Her biggest mistake is getting me vexed when man like Siobhan is in the crowd; having Siobhan here is like having my own energy source of power that's radiating onto me onstage. I look back at Moneypenny, this girl's going down. There are some boos from the crowd and the announcer gives Moneypenny an official warning, but she's still screwing when I win the coin toss and make her go first. The beat starts.

'I'm about to go up a level, until now I been chilling,

But this wasteman got me in the mood, now I'm feeling like winning.

This kid is so dumb they found him face down in a puddle, swimming.

How easy it is to battle such a freak, his boyfriend in the crowd looks like Carlton,

It's peak, I saw them kissing offstage and it weren't on the cheek.
Look at my YouTube, I got views for days,
I'm on track to end you, you're full of delays,
Finding ways to make the crowd like you, I despise you,
Your loser energy is stuck on like glue.
You're nothing and you'll stay there, I'm the new craze.
You little rat, you're the past, I'm the future,
You ain't coming back, you see me unfazed.
I been all over the world and I've seen nothing this whack,
My passport hardcore coz my lyrics, they bang,
I'll take you offline like a cyber attack,
Pooing your pants again until they're brown and they're black,
Despite the views of your poo, you can't do what I do,
Feel free to give it a crack.
With money like mine, we live in a house,
But I'll give you some pennies coz you live in a shack.'

OK, that was lit, but she's vexed me too much. When she rapped about me and Shanks, he's been through enough. Acting like she's some next hot thing. Fam, this what Mr Rix was talking about. She's got bars, but the way she's coming at me is basic, it's the same as everyone else onstage but with better lyrics. Mr Rix taught me to be different, that's the only way I'll send her packin' like she's Biggy waiting Tupac.

I don't even wait for the music to end. With a quick glance at Siobhan and the others to top up my invincible meter, I jump straight in.

'Moneypenny, your race is over, so tell me why you starting?

Taking shots for pity laughs but ain't nobody laughing.

I'm headed for the stratosphere and you know that you ain't going,

These lovely people wanted bars so why you keep 'em starving?

I'm lookin homeless but you a homophobe, you must be ashamed.

You accuse me of flopping, I can never be framed,

I frame paintings and I'm still road, but there's more to be gained.

Your views are viewed national but love travels the globe,

Yeah Shanks is my boy, I'll shout it from my megaphone,

In all those hard times he was never alone,

If he forgot to forgive, I could never atone,

Won't apply it to you for peakness you've shown.

See these bars off my brain, got no pressure, no strain,

Barricaded away and on the emptiest plain,

We move forward, art, music, family, freedom and I wanna explain this,

Yeah, I'll clear up my stains before I'm stating my changes.

You can stay ungrateful. Got a head like a grapefruit,

You taste untasteful, bitter, overrated, and I still don't rate you.

This that big debut and that big finale, you're falling,
Open your mouth, words come out but now the stars are calling.
So as for my rap game? Nah, I ain't stopping never
No frames, chains, planes or pains.
Yeah I'll be here forever.'

The music ends, and I feel kinda bad because the DJ had a bit of trouble keeping up at the beginning, there should have been a pause between our verses.

But the crowd is going wild. Everyone here, including all the other MCs and the media operators and the judges, is on their feet. I don't know if they're clapping me or Moneypenny, probably both. The judges seem to be discussing a lot more than they did with the previous battles, this is gonna be close.

A few moments go by, and then the host takes to the stage one last time.

'Let's give another round of applause for our two finalists!' She's bare enthusiastic. Everyone claps and screams and stomps their feet again. The announcer continues, 'MC Moneypenny, you battled hard, and not always clean, but you have lots of talent on the mic and we can't wait to see what you do next. But today's winner, thanks to his somewhat unique style of rapping, has to go to Shaun Thompson, AKA Growls Bethany Frenkel.' The crowd goes wild yet again, stamping their feet so much that the entire school hall feels like it's vibrating.

It's all too much. I get to stay in my house, I'm not getting evicted. My knees go wobbly, no one in here knows what this means to me. I saved my family. I get to stay with Shanks. Siobhan is here. I fought and I won.

Someone comes onstage with a giant cheque. It's like the ones you see in a lottery advert, there's no way the bank will accept it so I'm gonna ask for a smaller one later. But for now I pose with the big cheque for the flashing cameras. When I finally get down off the stage, people are patting me on the back as I head into the crowd, desperately scanning for Siobhan. I'll go and find the others later, but I'm scared Siobhan's gonna get dragged back to Bristol before I can find her. But before I can get very far, Moneypenny and her entourage step in front of me. For a second it looks like there's gonna be beef.

'Yo, Bethany, you were actually alright up there, you know. Let me know if you ever wanna hop on a track with me some time,' she says with her crew nodding along behind her. Bare thoughts go rushing through my mind of music videos and YouTube hits and popping bottles in the back of a limousine. Over her shoulder I see Shanks and Mr Rix chatting to my mum. Adrian is on his phone looking at the videos he just took of me onstage. Where is Siobhan?

Moneypenny is still chatting to me though, and I haven't

forgotten that she was so peak to Shanks for no reason. 'Yeah, the thing is, like, thanks for the offer and that, but I ain't about that life no more.' I wanna enjoy making music, I'm not tryna be popular online. We all know what can go wrong when I freestyle in front of a camera. And besides, I don't wanna make people feel bad just to make myself feel good. I guess in that way, Moneypenny still has a lot to learn. As she walks away I'm silently wishing her kind regards. But not best wishes, she'd probably waste those.

Bro, I still can't see Siobhan, but I do see Mr Rix coming over to me.

'Sir.' I run over, I have so much to tell him, so much to thank him for. This guy's lessons won me the competition. 'We did it, we won.'

'Your creativity did that. You listened, you learned, you applied. I want to see more of that next year.' I won't let him down.

He gives me a firm handshake, and says he has to shoot off, probably to do grown-up stuff like sort his taxes or bake some bread. I'm just grateful he came.

I catch Shanks' eye next and make my way towards him. Before either of us can talk, I give him the longest hug, and it feels like all the sadness at not seeing him all this time is just seeping out of me, like the hug is erasing all the pain of the last few months. Whether we're together or not, we're flying. There is still a split end that needs tying up though. I look around the crowd, desperately searching for a glimpse of her red hair. Did I imagine her?

'Shanks, bro, I thought I saw her. I think she's here.' I'm scanning the hall.

'Who? Siobhan?' He starts looking around, too. 'What does she look like?'

'What does she look like? She's the most beautiful girl ever. Her nails are chipped and when she smiles at you, it's like walking past the dry cleaners and you can smell the fresh laundry. She looks like an angel, and her eyes make you feel like you can do anything.' I don't think I can be any clearer with my description.

'And she has red hair?' Shanks asks.

'Yeah, she does.' Wait, I never told him she has red hair. Shanks is grinning. No way, please don't be playing with me . . .

I spin around on the spot and Siobhan is standing right there. She's been behind me the whole time. In my mind I picture the day we met in the basketball court, the way she laughed when we ate Italian food, the day in the art gallery when she made me believe in myself, the way she fell asleep on my shoulder during that terrible film and the day of the wedding when we slow-danced. I try to use words, but they just won't come.

'Hi,' she says, 'that was amazing, I've never actually heard you rap like that before. Can you do a rap about me one day?' She scratches the back of her neck like she's looking for something else to say.

'Fumblrb,' I reply. I was supposed to say 'hey, thanks for coming, yeah sure I got bars for you', but my voice doesn't work. It doesn't matter though, because out of nowhere, Siobhan grabs my face with both hands and kisses me right on the mouth. She lets go after a second, looking all embarrassed and that, and I think I'm gonna faint. I don't care that Adrian and Mum and Shanks are here, I am so gassed right now. This is like a dream. I wanna take off like a rocket, I really am a supernova.

'Oh Siobhan!' I exclaim. I close my eyes and open my mouth slightly as I lean in for round two, but my mum pulls me back by the collar.

'Boy, read the room,' she says, half laughing. 'Hi there.' She shakes Siobhan's hand and introduces herself and Adrian. He nods towards her, and wiggles his eyebrows at me. I pretend not to notice because Siobhan's standing right next to me and that's hella awks.

She grabs my hand and gives it a little squeeze.

'I have to go,' she says, walking backwards. 'I took my mum's card to get the train down, she doesn't know I'm here. I can't stay.' What? No! She can't go, she only just got here. Mum quietly tells Adrian and Shanks to give us some space.

'I don't get it. Please don't go. You haven't met Shanks

properly yet, and we didn't finish that film together, the anime one. Allow it, please stay, just for one day.'

'I'm sorry, Growls, I'm in enough trouble as it is. I really don't want to, but I have to go. It's not like anyone can volunteer in my place.' I wish someone could though, I wish I could find someone to take her place, like, someone who was a real life superhero. Like a volunteer superhero. A volunteer and a superhero. Like a charity person. Wait. Oh my God. Why didn't I think of this before?

'Siobhan, I need you to talk to someone.' I can feel her slipping away. 'Before you go, just please, please take my phone and talk to this person. If you don't get through, write it down and keep trying when you get home.' I have to try, I can't let her leave again without fighting for her, that ain't gonna happen. This is my last hope. I pull out my phone and start frantically scrolling down to Karen's number.

31

If It's Not Alright,
It's Not the End

We're having dinner in the kitchen, me, Mum and Adrian. The first thing I did when I got home was unpack my bags, because we're not going anywhere. Then I flopped down on my bed and lay with my hands behind my head. I let out a really long sigh, like I was blowing out birthday candles across the misty moors. At the dinner table, Mum chuckles as she says that it's been a long day, but I know that every day is at least twenty-four hours long. The maddest part is that Adrian's the one doing the cooking. Well, he put garlic bread and pizzas in the oven, and it actually turned out pretty decent. I didn't know how much I liked garlic bread #tastethetingle #sweetloaf #sweetchariot cauliflower to carry me home.

Even though we're celebrating Raptology, Mum's not

having it when I tell her that me and Adrian are gonna march down to Gregory Flynn's office as soon as we cash that cheque on Monday morning. When I ask her why not, Mum says she has some news to share with us. She's got a cheeky smile on her face and I don't know if I should be worried or excited.

'It's very sweet of you that you want to use your money for that, but you don't need to, because your useless old mum went and got herself a new job!' She squeals with excitement, and me and Adrian start cheering and banging our glasses with our forks. Apparently Mum was picking up more and more cleaning shifts, until Sharon came running over to tell her about an admin job that popped up in 'er 'usband 'arry's engineering company. She told Mum to email a CV over immediately, and Mum was on it. Now I think of it, I do remember when Sharon came over a few days ago, all red and sweaty and out of breath, but at the time I didn't make anything of it cause that's like her default setting. Mum didn't want to mention anything until it was in the bag though.

Can't lie, it's been tough the last few weeks, we had to cut back on a lot of things. Man was eating cereal with a fork in the morning to save on milk, and my toes keep popping out my socks like a tomato slice in a sandwich. It feels like it's just been me and Adrian in the house for a minute while she's been cleaning every hour of every day.

'Well, all that's about to change,' Mum says, and her voice is so big right now. 'The pay is much better. And I'm back on weekdays and daylight hours. And Adrian cooking? I could get used to this.' He looks embarrassed, but I know that deep down he's bare gassed. The golden balloon is inflating in my chest again and pushing tears out my eyes. My legs stand up and walk around the table and I fall into the biggest hug with my mum. She's stroking the back of my hair like that car journey, and whispering that she's so proud of me for what I did in Raptology and how much I've grown.

Adrian rolls his eyes and says, 'Swear on my life, you man are actually a problem,' and that just makes Mum laugh and do it even more.

Mr Rix was right, I guess we're all perfectly imperfect beautiful trees, and together we make a forest.

EPILOGUE

(not to be pronounced 'Epilogwe')

Yo, let me re-introduce myself. My name is Shaun Thompson, and the last few weeks have been a proper madness. We got to stay in the ends, and I didn't even have to use my Raptology money. Thanks to not having to pay for our house, I had enough P to get Mum a gift, something useful that she can use again and again. I did offer for her to have some of the money, but she told me to save it for when I go to university. So I got her a dancing flamingo that takes batteries and sings Yodelling songs whenever you walk past it. I saw it on Amazon and it goes crazy when anyone goes near it. It also doubles up as a punching bag, but I didn't know that when I bought it. Mum's so smart, she's always finding alternative uses for things.

When she went down to the housing office to sort out

the arrears, she found out that Gregory Flynn didn't tell us we could apply for an extension on the rent. Along with the new job, that extra week pretty much saved us. Mum's not balling or nothing though, she only just got the payments done in time. But with Sharon's help going through all the emails and texts and missed calls, Mum could prove that Gregory Flynn was guilty of harassment and reported him to the Senior Housing Officer. Apparently he called her almost ninety times in the space of two weeks, and even his co-workers grassed him up. I'm not sure if he lost his job, or got demoted, but either way he won't be troubling us any more. The night he said he was going to evict us, I stayed awake until the morning, thinking he was going to come back again. He never did.

Since then, Mum's been sticking to her word, spending more time around the house and that. I think she even inspired Adrian – he got a part-time job, which makes him even hungrier when he gets home for dinner. On the days he's really tired, Mum makes us all a hot chocolate before bed. And sometimes Adrian makes Mum a coffee in the morning or comes into my room to play FIFA, and we talk about what we've been up to that day. I do the shopping whenever I can, and once a week I try to cook Nanna's beef stew for both of them.

Shanks is back for good too, just like that song, and I'm over the flipping moon. It's almost like he never left. We're chilling in the studio today, and it's not like in the movies. It's a small room with a couch, just like my barbers, and another room next to it with a mic. The studio's in New Cross, so not too far, and there's a Jamaican bagel place across the road that's got cool graffiti on their shutters. Mr Rix once said that the area is gentrified, which is hypocritical because Mr Rix himself is super gentrified; he watches cricket games for fun, drinks mould wine and wears cardigans on purpose. For real, though, it's nice to be in a recording booth. I'm looking forward to making music. I'll put it out there, and if people listen then that's great, but if they don't then that's fine too.

Even though he's not about spitting bars any more Shanks tells me whether or not my bars bang. He's still my number-one hypeman. Right now he's scrolling on his phone, looking at pictures of Raptology. Everything is so calm, it's so easy having him about. We'll always be MC squared.

'You heard anything from Siobhan?' Shanks asks without looking up from his phone.

'She's got another video call today with her mum and the woman I told you about.'

We got hold of Karen after Raptology and explained the situation. Karen immediately got on the phone with her daughter, the one who runs the nursing charity, and they should be sorting things so Yvonne and Siobhan can get the care they need in their own home while they wait for the work to be done on the house. Apparently the chances are fifty-fifty, which makes me kinda nervous because that's almost half.

'Don't worry, bro, even if it don't work out, we can get the train up there every week, and holidays and that too.' This is why I love this guy. After all our time apart, we've grown, still, but some things stay the same. It's all love.

'Shanks, you're gonna love her. Swear down, if she does come next week, the first thing we'll do is all go out and get a Monday.' I can't wait.

Shanks puts his phone down and looks up, frowning.

'What the hell is a Monday?'

'You know, the ice cream. We'll go for an ice-cream Monday.'

'Bruh.' He shakes his head. 'Are you OK? You do realise it's called a "sundae". . . It's not named after the day of the week.' What is he on about? Why would they call it that otherwise? I'm pulling out my phone, Google will show him.

'Swear down, this guy.' Shanks laughs. 'You get one quick peck on the lips and suddenly you're moving all confident.'

'It wasn't a quick peck, it lasted several seconds. Several heavenly seconds. That's almost seven hours in dog years. It was like a Sundae, Mondae, Wednesdae, Fridae, Funday all rolled into one.'

'How are you gonna measure your first kiss in dog years

and then shout days of the week at me? Just finish your lyrics, fam.' We're both laughing, because yeah, I was clowning, but I really did miss him.

We spend the rest of the summer outside, going to parks and strolling through Southbank and that. There's a place where skaters go, and we like watching them fall over while we drink iced tea. I love this guy, he's my OG for life.

EPILOGUE

Part Two

This Time It's Personal

Me and Shanks are sitting in our English class, in our usual seats at the back by the window. I'm feeling positive about this new school year, the world is our oyster card. Shanks was nervous coming in, but we met at our usual spot near the bus stop, and no one's started any beef. If anything, they're kinda welcoming, a bit like when Messi went to PSG, out of the goodness of his heart and his love for Paris and his £480,000 per week wages.

'Why you keep looking at the door?' Shanks is asking.

'Why *do* you keep looking at the door?' I correct him.

'Allow me, see this is what happens when you learn stuff.'

'I love you, bro.' I'm not even afraid to say it any more.

'I love you too. But seriously, you keep looking over there. Calm down, she'll be here soon.'

Just then, a familiar, pretty face walks into the classroom, and my heart starts beating proper fast like electro doof-doof music. Tanisha's arrived, and she's surrounded by her friends. But I wait for them to sit down and get out the way because Siobhan walks in just behind them. Her hair looks redder than it's ever been, like a phoenix rising from the ashes. She's wearing our school uniform, and it looks so wavey on her, which is funny because on the phone last night she told me she was nervous about wearing it. But what if Martin Luther was nervous? He would have never made those old school bangers, and he probably wouldn't drive a van dross. Shanks gives her a little wave to tell her where we are. I'm on my feet, waving my arms like a maniac in case she doesn't see us.

Turns out Karen's daughter really is a superhero because she sorted everything out to get Siobhan and Yvonne help. I was crying on the phone when Siobhan told me they were moving back. Yo, shout-out Karen and Karen Junior, you know! Now, carers go round every morning and afternoon to help with shopping and cooking and that. And now Siobhan finally has the freedom to attend school during the day. And guess what school she chose?

Her and Shanks don't know each other super well, but we've got the whole school year to fix that. First chance we get, we're gonna go and shoot some hoops in the cage near my yard.

Siobhan takes the empty seat next to me and I feel like I'm in heaven. I got my two best friends in the whole world and I can't wait for our next adventures. I look at Shanks, and I look at Siobhan (she's so beautiful when she rummages through her pencil case).

Mr Rix comes in then, telling everyone to settle down. He looks over and sees Siobhan and Shanks either side of me. No one notices, but he nods at me, and I nod back. He begins the lesson.

BONUS TRACK

I weren't ready for this, I was steady for this,
Making waves like the queen, gotta steady the ship.
Gotta ride that wave like tidal, lyrics non-vital,
Until death doo-doo part and my poo-pants went viral.
Yo, Shanks was gone for a minute
That madness online got him pushed to the limit
Shout-out Karen and Rix for keeping me with it.
Got my mum by my side like a side dish of spinach,
Where there's a wheel there's a way no matter how hard
you spin it.
Made up with Adrian who once got me wetting my bedding.
Getting into the mind of an artist took some imagery
shedding,
Shedding the shade, the front and the hype,

Couldn't stomach my ways like cow foot and tripe.
Yeah, shooting hoops in the cage, love made me act the fool,
Trash at the game but I was playin' it cool,
All heart, art, moves, bars, man's listing things Siobhan's impressed with.
Wasn't keen on Costa but now I'm invested
Italian followed, would've choked on that olive with that stone if I swallowed,
Circumstances left a hole in me like a bagel, hollowed,
But lip-balm friends got me back into hot mode when I wallowed.
That night at Siobhan's I know Yvonne got it right,
You get rid of darkness by introducing the light
The two both exist, the artist chooses the fight.

Author's Note

Alone in my tiny flat in Peckham, during the pandemic lockdown, I was re-enacting scenes from *Tangled* and making paper sunglasses with an online origami tutorial. That was week one. In week two I wrote the first draft of *Steady for This*.

Flashback . . .

At university a couple years earlier, I'd written the first three chapters, but those lockdown weeks gave me the chance to finish. My friend Jack would drag me to the library, and my tutors gave me the formula to write (show don't tell, remember your narrative arcs, etc). Even in its earliest stages of conception, I've never been in this alone. Criticism helped me to grow.

Flashback even more . . .

. . . to me reading as a kid. I loved reading, but there were never really any diverse characters, at least none that I could relate to.

Growing up and going to school in Peckham as an ethnic minority, the connotation was always that we were troubled, unruly kids with difficult lives. Stories that were set 'on the block' were depicted as gritty and dark. But in reality we were honestly very happy, we hung out and we laughed all day. I wrote *Steady For This* with the dream that kids like me might see themselves represented in a positive and authentic way. I picture kids who have never seen themselves in literature finally enjoy reading funny stories from the world in which they live.

And if any aspiring authors are reading this, I would suggest that you just read and write as much as you can, and take chances. The worst-case scenario is that life goes on. Best case is that a great agent makes a deal with wonderful publishers who pay you for telling a story. It's not a dream, it's a reality, that you can be a writer, no matter your background or postcode.

My advice would be to listen and to trust that there are stories all around you. I will always be an aspiring author, and I'll always hope that untold stories find their way into the light.

Acknowledgements

There's no 'I' in teaim. There is absolutely no way this book would be what it is without a ton of people.

They say it takes five people to make the perfect strawberry jam, and if people be the strawberry of this book, then jam, jam on.

If your name is on this list, give yourself a pat on the forehead:

Teresa for selflessly gifting me the laptop

Obviously OGC – aka Clare Wallace at Darley Anderson, akaka my extraordinary agent akakaka Throne Smasher

All the heads at Bonnier and Hot Key that have given me life
Ruth and Ella, big man ting – my editors, my safety net, my friends, you bow to no one
Rob with the marketing, AI with the braids
Talya for taking the time like Kang the Conqueror
Sophie McDonnell who designed the cover with art by

Yone Welsch. For all of you who judge a book by its cover artist – this guy is amazing, check out his IG: @yone_welsch

The Defence Attorneys at the DA office of the Darley Anderson Agency:
Rosanna the Purse Keeper
Lydia the Brave
Chloe the not Kardashian
Kristina the Local Ally
Becca the Best of US, she walks here and there, to thunderous applause

First readers:
Sara for championing my work #bestiebro
Abs LeKendeh on the commute, thanks for the honesty
Benj for megalols
Uncle Gwi-gwi
Jonathan and his new eyes
Manon, Seb, Judy, Josh, in no particular order, especially not alphabetical
Jack Walsh for the input
Fred for the musical input
International cousins Elena and Adrian

The real Mr Rix. Wherever he is, I know he's happy for me. I know this because he's teaching my cousin at a school in South London, we're still in contact. Let's grab a drink soon.

Adrian for being the voice of Growls
James for the production
Eni for being ridiculous
Tim and Tara for giving me a place to write

Alice and the staff at Queensbridge School, you are born teachers (technically born babies but most humans are)
    Shout-out Tayme and Harry, your stories will change lives. Never forget that.

Helena Blakemore
Tessa Mcwatt
Tim Atkins
For teaching me to write. The student has become the pupil.

To my agency siblings:
JP Rose, Ayaan Mohamud, Beth Reekles, Polly Ho-Yen – they say that dreams come true when the sky accepts the turtle dove. May our doves walk in the fields of freedom shine yes (OK that one makes no sense but the sentiment is there)

* * *

And to the reader, I thank you for reading this. I sincerely hope you've been entertained. They say in life the most mysterious sentences . . .

Nathanael Lessore

Nathanael Lessore was born in Camberwell, South East London, as one of eight children to French and Madagascan parents. Despite spending most of his life in Peckham, Nathanael has also lived in Paris, Strasbourg and Singapore. Nathanael became a marketing executive after graduating from the University of East London, believing at the time that a creative-writing degree destined him for a career in marketing. Nathanael can run 100 metres in under 10 minutes and has trouble finding sunglasses that frame his face properly. *Steady for This* is his debut and writing it gave him the opportunity to show his South East London childhood as the funny, warm, adventurous world that wasn't always represented as such.

If you liked **STEADY FOR THIS,** you'll love **KING OF NOTHING!**

From Yoto Carnegie Medal-shortlisted author Nathanael Lessore